DUKE ELLINGTON

"I Live With Music"

Carin T. Ford

Series Consultant:
Dr. Russell L. Adams, Chairman
Department of
Afro-American Studies,
Howard University

Enslow Publishers, Inc.
40 Industrial Road
Box 398
Berkeley Heights, NJ 07922
USA
http://www.enslow.com

"I Live With Music."
—Duke Ellington

Copyright © 2008 by Carin T. Ford

Library of Congress Cataloging-in-Publication Data

Ford, Carin T.
    Duke Ellington : "I live with music" / by Carin T. Ford.
      p. cm.— (African-American biography library)
    Includes bibliographical references and index.
    ISBN-13: 978-0-7660-2702-2
    ISBN-10: 0-7660-2702-3
    1. Ellington, Duke, 1899–1974—Juvenile literature. 2. Jazz musicians—United States—Biography—Juvenile literature. 3. African-American musicians—Biography—Juvenile literature. I. Title. II. Series.
    ML3930.E44F67 2007
    781.65092—dc22
    [B]
                                        2006013794

Printed in the United States of America
112009 Lake Book Manufacturing, Inc., Melrose Park, IL

10 9 8 7 6 5 4 3 2

Illustration Credits: Associated Press, pp. 116, 118; Bettman/Corbis, p. 81; Bill Lebovich, p. 20; Chicago Historical Society, Chicago Daily News negatives collection, #SDN-001413, p. 6; Duke Ellington Collection, Archives Center, National Museum of American History, Behring Center, Smithsonian Institution, pp. 3, 5 (center and left), 10 (center and left), 11, 23 (center and left), 29, 35 (center and left), 39, 46 (center and left), 58 (center and left), 69 (center and left), 83 (center and left), 98 (center and left), 107 (center and left); Edward and Gayle Ellington Collection, Archives Center, National Museum of American History, Behring Center, Smithsonian Institution, p. 14; Everett Collection, Inc., pp. 4, 52, 56, 105; Frank Driggs Collection/Getty Images, pp. 49, 66, 71, 75; The Granger Collection, New York, pp. 43, 84; "Howard Theatre at Night" by Mary Belcher of Washington, D.C., published with permission of the artist, p. 27; Hulton Archive/Getty Images, p. 79; © 2006 Jupiterimages Corporation, p. 62; Lebrecht Music & Arts/Image Works, p. 64; Library of Congress, Prints and Photographs Division, pp. 5 (right), 7, 10 (right), 23 (right), 35 (right), 46 (right), 58 (right), 69 (right), 83 (right), 89, 98 (right), 107 (right); Library of Congress, Rare Books and Special Collections Division, p. 68; Metronome/Getty Images, p. 91; Nicholas Kamm/AFP/Getty Images, p. 25; Photofest, p. 96; Time Life Pictures/Getty Images, p. 109; Wikipedia.org, p. 17; William P. Gottlieb/Ira and Lenore S. Gershwin Fund Collection, Music Division, Library of Congress, pp. 103.

Cover Illustrations: Everett Collection, Inc. (top); Getty Images (bottom).

Contents

Duke Ellington was a composer and a musician
and did his best work on the piano.

◆ ◆ ◆ ◆ ◆

Chapter 1

Doing It His Way

Edward Ellington preferred baseball to just about any other activity. He liked playing the game with his school friends, and he especially enjoyed watching his hometown major league team, the Senators, play at Griffith Stadium in Washington, D.C.

His mother, Daisy Ellington, worried a lot about her only child. She was a protective mother, always afraid that Edward might get hurt—and one day he did.

Edward was playing baseball with friends at school. During the game, a boy was swinging a bat. By accident, he smacked Edward in the back of the head. Daisy Ellington had been standing nearby and immediately took Edward to see a doctor.

Edward recovered, but Daisy worried that baseball was too rough for her son. She wanted him to become

Edward Ellington loved watching the Washington Senators (above) and playing baseball, but his mother wanted him to play the piano.

◆ ◆ ◆ ◆ ◆

interested in another activity. So she signed him up for piano lessons.

Edward was supposed to take a few lessons each week, but he did not show up for most of them. He enjoyed running around with his friends and playing baseball more than he liked sitting at the piano with his teacher, Marietta Clinkscales. "Half the time she'd come around and I'd be out there playing baseball or something, my mother had to pay her off," said Edward.[1]

When the teacher held a recital at the local church, Edward was the only student who was not able to play his part.

Piano became even less important to Edward as he grew older. He took a job selling peanuts, popcorn, and candy at the baseball park. This way, he was able to see all the Senators games for free. The piano did not seem to have a place in Edward's life. Even in school, he took a special interest in drawing and painting, but not music.

The summer before Edward started high school, he took a vacation with his mother to Asbury Park, New Jersey. He decided to look for a job at one of the hotels along the Atlantic Ocean. He heard of an opening for a dishwasher and was hired for the position. Edward had

When he was young, Edward Ellington got a job
near the beach at Asbury Park.

◆◆◆◆◆◆◆◆◆◆◆◆◆◆◆◆◆◆◆◆◆◆◆

Learning From People, Not Lessons

Edward took lessons with several piano players, but he was not able to learn from them. He did not like being told what to do. He believed that taking lessons destroyed a person's natural musical ability. Edward would turn away from formal musical training throughout his life. Yet he was able to learn by spending time with some outstanding musicians. For example, Edward worked with Will Vodrey, who headed a big brass band. Edward watched Vodrey carefully and later said he received "valuable lessons in orchestration" from the bandleader."[2]

never washed dishes before. A man named Bowser, who had been working at the hotel for a year, showed Edward how to scrub the dishes properly, and the two became friends.

Bowser told Edward about a wonderful young piano player who lived in Philadelphia, Pennsylvania. His name was Harvey Brooks, and he was just about Edward's age. When the summer came to an end, Edward had to leave Asbury Park and head back to Washington. Bowser suggested that on the way, they stop off in Philadelphia, where they could hear Brooks play.

It was an experience that changed Edward's life. "He was swinging and he had a tremendous left hand, and when I got home I had a real yearning to play," Edward said. "I hadn't been able to get off the ground before, but after hearing him I said to myself, 'Man, you're just going to *have* to do it.'"[3]

With little formal training, Edward did it—and he did it his way. He listened, watched, and learned. One day, long after he had been given the nickname Duke, he would be considered one of the most important names in American music in the twentieth century.

Chapter 2

Between Music and Art

Edward Kennedy Ellington was born April 29, 1899, in Washington, D.C. His birth certificate says that he was Daisy and James Ellington's second child. Yet there is no record of Edward's older brother or sister. The Ellington's first child may have died in infancy.

Edward moved many times throughout the northwestern section of Washington. Wherever he and his parents lived, it was always in the better area of the African-American section of the nation's capital. For the most part, he lived in middle-class neighborhoods, where his neighbors were teachers and government workers.

Daisy and James Ellington cared about living in a good neighborhood. They wanted to have nice furniture and dishes in their home. James had been born in North

Daisy Ellington wanted the best for her children. This portrait of her has an inscription from her to her nephew in the lower left corner. It is unknown whose signature is in the lower right corner.

Carolina in 1879. He lived with his parents and numerous brothers and sisters on a farm and received more of an education than most black children in the South. Although the Civil War had ended fourteen years before James was born, life was not easy for African Americans in the South at that time. Not only were they treated unfairly, but lynchings—in which mobs would hunt down and kill African Americans—were common. When James was a teenager, he decided to head north to Washington, D.C., with some of his brothers.

James Ellington was able to find work, and he held several jobs. He worked as a waiter and drove a coach. He also went to work for M. F. Cuthburt, a doctor who cared for the wealthy people in the area. James Ellington took a position as the doctor's coachman but later became the Cuthburt family's butler. It was at this time that he met Daisy Kennedy. James Ellington spoke well and had an elegant, polite way about him—qualities Edward would inherit. James acted as if he were as wealthy as the people he worked for. "He spent and lived like a man who had money," Edward said about his father, "and he raised his family as though he were a millionaire."[1]

Daisy Kennedy was born in Washington, D.C., the same year as her husband. Yet her background was quite different. Her father was captain of the police, and her family was wealthier than James'. She was a well-educated, religious woman with strong values.

Daisy Kennedy and James Ellington married in 1898. Edward was born one year later. He was their only child until he turned sixteen and his sister, Ruth, was born. Although Daisy and James had their differences, they both wanted their son and later, their daughter, too, to have the best of everything. They saw to it that Edward grew up in a neighborhood where people lived in three-story brick houses and had trees in their yards. James Ellington had become friendly with the Cuthbert family and often was given pieces of china and silverware, which he then used in his own home. He also was able to bring home steaks and seafood from occasional jobs as a caterer. Several times he worked as a butler for events at the White House.

James and Daisy made sure Edward learned good manners, how to dress properly, and how to speak well. Each Sunday, Daisy took her son to two services—one at the Baptist church she belonged to and another at her husband's Methodist church. She enrolled her son in Sunday school and taught him that God had no color. "My mother started telling me about God when I was very young," Ellington said later. "There was never any talk about red people, brown people, black people, or yellow people, or about the differences that existed between them."[2] Years later, Ellington said that by the time he turned thirty, he had read the whole Bible four times.

Edward's mother told him many times that he was blessed, and he believed her. Edward was raised to feel

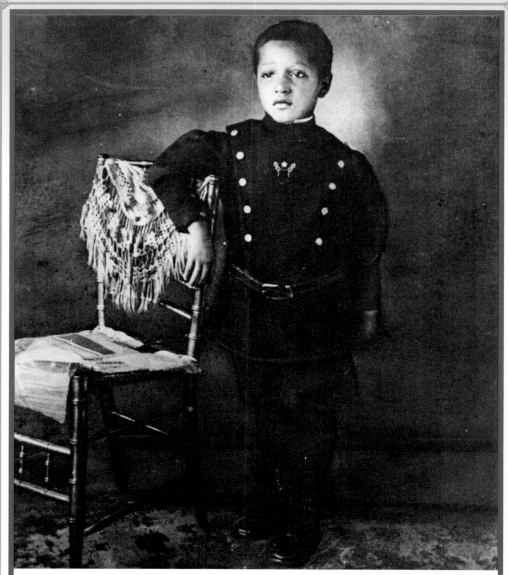

Daisy Ellington made sure Edward knew how to dress properly.
In this studio portrait, he is four years old.

confident about himself. "I was pampered and pampered, and spoiled rotten," he said.[3]

Although Daisy had strong morals, James Ellington enjoyed flirting with women. He loved to dance and joke and flatter, all qualities his son would imitate. Even though Edward was not interested in taking music lessons as a young boy, he grew up listening to both his parents play the piano. James played arias—songs from operas—while Daisy preferred playing popular songs and ragtime.

Edward started out at Patterson Elementary School when he was five years old and moved on to Garnet Elementary School at age seven or eight. There, baseball was his chief interest. He also enjoyed the theater and by age eleven—without his mother's knowing about it—he would sneak into the Gayety Theater to see burlesque shows. These were live variety shows performed onstage with comedy, dancing, and striptease. Edward also visited the Howard Theater, the first large theater for African Americans in the nation's capital, and Frank Holliday's poolroom, which located a few blocks from the Ellingtons' house.

At the poolroom, Edward mixed with a variety of people, including students, doctors, waiters, and piano players. Many local pianists came to the poolroom, and Edward was always interested in hearing them play.

By the time he entered high school in 1913, Edward planned to study commercial art at the Armstrong Manual

Training School. He seemed to have a talent for art. The Armstrong School appeared to be a good choice for his interests and abilities, rather than the more academic M Street High School, the country's first public high school for African Americans.

Even though Edward did not want to take piano lessons, he continued to enjoy listening to piano music. His favorite kind of music was ragtime. Ragtime piano began back in the late 1800s and attracted both black and white listeners—the first African-American music to do so. Ragtime had an upbeat sound with a steady bass part and a faster-paced, bouncy melody. Although rags were not considered jazz, they helped develop the jazz sound, especially for the piano. One of the most famous ragtime composers was Scott Joplin, who wrote "Maple Leaf Rag," among other pieces. Young people seemed drawn to ragtime, and Edward was no exception.

When Edward heard the young pianist Harvey Brooks perform on the piano in Philadelphia that summer, his interest in music firmly took root. He said, "I said right then, 'That's how I would like to play a piano.'"[4]

One day he sat down at the piano in his home—this time, without his mother telling him to do so—and began to play around with the notes, experimenting with different melodies. He did not remember much that his teacher, Mrs. Clinkscales, had taught him. Instead, he played by ear, sounding out the notes without reading any sheet

This cover of the sheet music for "Maple Leaf Rag"
has a picture of the composer, Scott Joplin. Joplin's ragtime
tunes had an early influence on Edward Ellington.

music. Soon, he was able to listen to a song and not only reproduce it but perform it with his own variations.

At the age of fourteen, he wrote a piece called "Soda Fountain Rag," also called "Poodle Dog Rag," named for his experience working at the Poodle Dog Café. He continued listening to the pianists who came to Holliday's poolroom and based his own music on the rags and popular songs he heard them perform.

Edward worked on the "Soda Fountain Rag," constantly revising and perfecting it, though he never wrote down the notes on paper. He went on to compose more pieces, such as "What You Gonna Do When the Bed Breaks Down?" This second song had a slow tempo compared to the fast-paced "Soda Fountain Rag." Edward's friends enjoyed his compositions, and he kept at it.

At this time, his good friend Edgar McEntree gave Edward the nickname that would stay with him throughout his life. Because of Edward's polished manners and fashionable way of dressing, McEntree called him "Duke."

During his years in high school, Duke Ellington played the piano at parties and dances. Because he needed more than two songs when performing at these events, Duke took the compositions he had already written and rearranged them. By changing the tempo, he found that the same basic melody could be rewritten as a waltz, a tango, and a fox-trot. His listeners thought he was playing a variety of songs. The truth was, most of his compositions at this time were based on just a few melodies.

Duke not only enjoyed making music, he also liked the popularity that came with being a pianist. Young women flocked to his side when he sat at the piano. Duke was like his father—he enjoyed the attention.

Duke's musical ability continued to improve because of the time he spent with piano players at the poolroom. There, Duke had the best of both worlds. He was exposed to pianists who had been formally trained at music conservatories along with those who were self-taught and simply played by ear.

"There were things I wanted to do that were not in books," he said, "and I had to ask a lot of questions. I was lucky enough to run into people who had the answers."[5]

Duke learned from them all. The "ear cats," as he called them, included Clarence Bowser, Sticky Mack, and Blind Johnny.

Learning on His Own

Duke was happy working on his own. It seemed as if he did better when left to his own devices, instead of studying with a teacher. In high school, for example, he received a grade of D in the one music class he took. Yet often he would skip classes so that he could play the piano in the school's gym. As for the other subjects he studied, Duke was not an especially good student. The only decent grades he earned were in freehand and mechanical drawing.

Duke spent most of his teenage years
in this home in Washington, D.C.

Among the "schooled guys" were Louis Brown, Louis Thomas, and most important, Oliver "Doc" Perry.[6] "I used to go up to Doc Perry's house almost every day, sit there in a flow of enchantment, until he'd pause and explain some passage," said Duke. "He had the patience to share with me his theories and observations."[7]

Duke referred to Perry as his "piano parent." From Perry he learned how to identify chords and read the lead. This way he could play the melody with his right hand and form chords with his left hand. "Even if I didn't learn to play it, I knew how it was done," Duke said.[8]

Perry did not charge any money for his time, plus he gave Duke something to eat and drink as they worked. Occasionally, Perry asked Duke to take his place at the afternoon dances that were held during the week. This led to jobs as a temporary substitute for other pianists who performed at African-American nightclubs and cafés in the Washington, D.C., area.

When Duke turned seventeen, he finally was forced to choose between music and art. He had entered—and won—a contest to design a poster for the National Association for the Advancement of Colored People (NAACP). His prize was a scholarship to the Pratt Institute of Applied Arts in Brooklyn, New York, where he

> When Duke turned seventeen, he finally was forced to choose between music and art.

would study art. Duke looked upon his skill as an artist as a talent, while he considered his musical ability to be more of a gift. He was earning decent money at the time playing the piano, and he decided to turn down the scholarship.

The following year, Duke made another decision. With only three months remaining until his graduation, he dropped out of high school. He worked during the day as a sign painter. In the evening, he played the piano.

Chapter 3

Putting It Together

Though he was only a teenager, Edward "Duke" Ellington went into a partnership with Ewell Conaway in a sign-painting business. He also launched his career as a professional musician, playing piano at True Reformers Hall. He played for five hours and received seventy-five cents for his efforts. "This was my first gig and I ran home like a thief with that money," he said.[1]

Ellington began playing piano regularly in the evenings, working with such bandleaders as Louis Thomas and Russell Wooding. Meanwhile, he continued painting signs during the day.

"He was always ambitious and needed very little sleep," said his sister, Ruth Ellington.[2]

There were some difficulties in the beginning. Ellington liked to do things his way. Unlike the rest of the musicians, he did not always dress properly. He also strayed from the piano music that was written, instead playing his own arrangement. So the band fired him.

When Ellington was about eighteen years old, he decided to put together his own musical group. The band, called Duke's Serenaders, was made up of Ellington on piano along with a drummer, a saxophone player, and a guitarist or banjo player. The band played frequently at the True Reformers Hall from eight at night until the early hours of the morning. Ellington and his mother were very proud of the seventy-five cents he earned from each dance engagement. The Serenaders played ragtime, blues, and popular songs of the day.

"Just being together, playing together, was all that mattered then," said Otto "Toby" Hardwick, the band's sax player. "There wasn't any money involved, not to speak of."[3]

Under Ellington's leadership, the band thrived. Although he was only a teenager, Ellington moved out of his parents' home and lived on his own. To help advertise his band, Ellington took out an ad in the classified section of the telephone directory, listing himself as manager: "Irresistible Jass," it read, "Furnished to our select patrons. The Duke's Serenaders, colored syncopaters, E. K. Ellington, mgr."[4] (Back then, "jazz" was often spelled "jass.") Included in the ad were his address and phone number.

Today, True Reformers Hall, where Ellington got his start, is called True Reformer Building and boasts a mural of Ellington on one of its walls. The mural was painted by artist Byron Peck and local high school students.

Ellington had invested some money in a telephone in order to help get jobs.

The ad attracted attention. Playing for both black and white crowds, the Serenaders became a popular band. The group played at balls that were held after horse shows and also frequently performed at embassies and large private estates.

Ellington focused on the music, but he also took charge of all the business arrangements. He landed jobs for the Serenaders outside the Washington area and put together other bands that used his name but did not include him. Some nights he had five bands performing throughout the Baltimore, Maryland, and Washington, D.C., area. He still worked at his job painting signs, and whenever he was asked to paint one for an upcoming dance, he would ask who was providing the music. He found many jobs for his band this way.

By this time, Ellington was earning enough money to afford a car and a house. He had been dating a school friend, Edna Thompson, for about two years. Edna had grown up in the same neighborhood and came from a family of teachers and principals. The two had fallen in love during high school. They got married on July 2, 1918. On March 11, 1919, they had a son and named him Mercer Kennedy Ellington. The family lived on Sherman Avenue in Washington. Soon Edna became pregnant again, but the baby died in infancy.

At this time, Ellington began studying music with Henry Grant, a high school music teacher. Grant also played piano as a soloist as well as with a trio that performed classical music.

Two times a week, Ellington visited Grant's house, where he learned harmony and also worked on his ability to read music. Ellington and his musicians began to play regularly before the main show at the well-known Howard

This illustration of the Howard Theater, called "Howard Theatre at Night," was done by Mary Belcher.

Theater. The musicians also were hired to play for dances around the city, both indoors and out.

Another popular type of music at this time was stride— or shout—piano. Stride piano was influenced by ragtime, but stride had a more distinct swing rhythm and allowed the pianist to improvise, or make up, sections of a song as he or she played. Stride had an *oompah* sound in the left hand and a structure that was like a march. One of the most famous pieces by James P. Johnson, a well-known stride pianist, was called "Carolina Shout." Ellington was fascinated by the song when he heard it on a piano roll. Piano rolls were popular in the early 1900s. Each roll of paper had holes punched in it—one hole for every piano key. The roll moved over a tracker bar inside the player piano, which reproduced the sound of each note. Songs could be listened to over and over.

Ellington listened to "Carolina Shout" at a friend's house. After hearing it the first time, he returned each day to listen to it again. He asked his friend to play the piano roll at a slower tempo so he could see which keys on the piano were moving. Watching the player piano, he could see each individual key of the piano move. Soon, Ellington was able to play the difficult piece from memory.

The following year, Johnson came to Washington, D.C., to play in a jazz show. He performed "Carolina Shout," and when Ellington's friends heard the piece, they urged Ellington to sit down at the piano and perform it for

Johnson after the show. Ellington was scared. Not only was Johnson older and a very well-respected musician throughout the country, but this was the piece of music he had made famous.

"I was scared stiff, but James P. was not only a master, he was also a great man for encouraging youngsters," Ellington said.[5]

Ellington, center, poses with his band in 1920.

Ellington gathered his courage and sat down to play the piece. Johnson applauded him heartily when he was done and Ellington spent the rest of the evening listening to the older musician. "What I absorbed on that occasion might, I think, have constituted a whole semester in a conservatory," Ellington said.[6]

Since first becoming interested in music, Ellington had looked for musicians who were more skilled than he was. Just as he had stood by the sides of Doc Perry and Harvey Grant, Ellington now spent time with Johnson, standing next to him at the piano and intently studying his technique. Ellington had never been interested in formal musical training. Instead, he preferred choosing what he wanted to learn and then learning it at his own pace.

Ellington broadened and developed his own technique and style by participating in band competitions. Jazz bands frequently competed against each other, with audience members betting on which band would be the best. Ellington often led his own musicians in these contests. He learned a lot about music and the art of pleasing an audience from these experiences.

Ellington traveled around the East Coast, always eager to hear new bands and top piano players. He also became eager to expand beyond the Washington area. Ellington had not enjoyed school or taking formal music lessons, but he was not afraid of hard work. All his life, he would push himself to be the best. William "Sonny" Greer would help push him in the right direction.

Greer, a drummer, had been drawn to Ellington since their first meeting. "From the moment I was introduced to Duke, I loved him," said Greer. "It was just something about him. He didn't know it, but he had it then."[7]

Greer had connections with people in the music business in New York City. In early 1923, he received an offer to work as the drummer for Wilbur Sweatman's band in the city. Sweatman had first performed in a circus band before getting into vaudeville—turn-of-the-century entertainment that included music, dancing, and comedy acts. Sweatman went on to form his own successful orchestra, first in Chicago and then in New York. Greer told Sweatman he would play only if Ellington were included as well (along with Otto "Toby" Hardwick, a bass and saxophone player).

At first, Ellington was not sure what to do. He had made a name for himself in Washington and lived a very comfortable life there. In addition, Washington was where his family lived. However, Ellington knew that for a musician—especially a jazz musician—New York was the place to be, particularly Harlem. A smart, confident man, Ellington had a way of winning people over, and he was not afraid of challenges. He decided to go.

The Harlem Renaissance

Duke Ellington arrived in New York City just before he turned twenty-four. Harlem thrilled him. Its African-American population was even larger than Washington's. Between 1920 and 1930, the number of African-American residents more than doubled in Harlem. The area was going through what later would be called the Harlem Renaissance. African-American musicians, artists, and writers were turning out creative work that all people—regardless of skin color—enjoyed. African-American music was flourishing and Harlem attracted the best musicians.

"Harlem, to our minds, did indeed have the world's most glamorous atmosphere," he said. "We had to go there."[8]

Ellington began playing with Sweatman's band in March 1923. The group was part of a vaudeville show, and Ellington learned a lot about show business from the experience. Sweatman had been hired to play for one week. When the week was over, Ellington, Greer, and Hardwick decided to remain in New York and look for work there. But this turned out to be more difficult than they expected.

"We rehearsed for a while, and rehearsed some more— but nothing much really happened," said Greer. "We had to get going on the rounds of the clubs, carrying our horns. Sometimes there'd be tips and that way we existed—after a fashion, everything divided three ways."[9]

Ellington was new to the area and did not have a reputation; no one had heard of him. Also, the competition among musicians in New York was very stiff. To earn money, the musicians played and bet on pool during the day. After earning a few dollars, they would buy food and then spend the evening visiting one club after another, hoping to get hired. They had no place of their own to live. Instead, they spent the nights with different relatives who lived in New York.

Although Ellington was earning very little money, he was learning all the time. Because of his good manners, fashionable clothes, and natural charm, he became acquainted with the well-known pianists in Harlem, and they liked him. Ellington was allowed to hang around the piano players at different clubs and occasionally, he would get a chance to perform.

"There was some sort of magnetism to him you wouldn't understand," Greer said. "In my whole life, I've never seen another man like him. When he walks into a strange room, the whole place lights up."[10]

One way in which Ellington was able to earn money was by playing at rent parties. These parties were held nearly every weekend in Harlem. Many people living in apartments had difficulty coming up with the money to pay the monthly rent. So they would throw a rent party. Often, more than a hundred people would pile into an apartment, each person paying an admission price of up to one dollar, with another twenty-five cents for a drink. The guests were served food and could enjoy listening to piano music. The renter used whatever was left over toward that month's rent. Prohibition had been in effect since 1920, when a law was passed making it illegal to sell alcoholic drinks. The fact that alcoholic drinks were served at these rent parties helped draw large crowds.

For Ellington the parties meant free food and a salary of about a dollar, a little over eleven dollars by today's standards. With the dollar Ellington earned from a rent party, he could buy lunch the next day and still have money left over. During his early days in Harlem, Ellington performed at rent parties every Saturday night.

Living in Harlem was a daily struggle. One day Ellington found $15 lying in the street. "Then we had a square meal, got on the train, and went back to Washington to get ourselves together before we tried it again," he said.[11]

When Ellington arrived back in Washington, he was certainly no richer than when he left. As usual, though, he had listened and he had watched. He had paid careful attention to the musicians who had successful careers. He would take all that he had learned and use it in years to come.

Chapter 4

Back in New York

Ellington was able to slip back easily into his old life in Washington. He started painting signs and playing music around the area again. He was able to spend time with his wife and son as well.

In June 1923, Ellington returned to New York. Greer and Hardwick, along with Elmer Snowden and Arthur Whetsol, asked Ellington to come back to the city, practically guaranteeing that this time they would find work for him. Ellington knew that New York City was the place a musician needed to be, and he was more than willing to try his luck there once again.

"Because I had a gig waiting for me, I felt entitled to travel in style. I hopped a train, took a parlor car, ate a big, expensive dinner in the diner, and got a cab at Pennsylvania Station to take me uptown. . . . I had spent all my money by the time I reached 129th Street," he said.[1]

Ellington and his musicians spent that hot summer auditioning in New York. One day, they visited the big amusement park in Coney Island. There, said Hardwick, a fortune teller told the young musicians, "You're thinking of going back home, don't do it. Something's going to break for you in 3 days and you fellows will work together for the rest of your lives and never have to look for a job again!"[2]

The musicians were finally hired to perform at the Music Box in Atlantic City, New Jersey. The band's luck changed when they were asked to play at the Exclusive Club, a popular nightclub in Harlem patronized mostly by white customers.

"We'd got our feet on the first rung of the ladder," said Hardwick. "It seems they liked us. Our music was different, even then. We were only five, but we had arrangements on everything. It was sort of conversation music, soft yet gut-bucket."[3]

The band was being paid a salary in addition to earning about $30 in tips each night. Ellington felt confident enough to send for his wife, Edna. Young Mercer remained in Washington with Ellington's parents.

When a cabaret—a kind of nightclub—opened next door to the Lafayette Theatre, Ellington was hired as the pianist. It was his job to play during the daytime rehearsals for the acts that would be performing onstage at night.

Ellington also was trying to sell some of his compositions. Working with an African-American lyricist (a person who writes the words, or lyrics, to a song), Ellington visited various publishers and auditioned some of his songs. But that summer of 1923, no one was interested.

In the fall of 1923, when Ellington was twenty-four years old, he played with the Black Sox Orchestra at the Hollywood Club. Elmer Snowden was the leader of the band, which included Ellington, Greer, Hardwick, and Whetsol. The club was small and bare and could hold only about one hundred people. Yet it had an excellent location near Times Square and was a popular club. This job lasted

Charm and Determination

Ellington's calm, polite manner often hid the very ambitious and hardworking man underneath. In July 1923, he made his first recording with Snowden's Novelty Orchestra. The following month, leading a band featuring a blues singer, Ellington made a radio broadcast. Ellington was determined to make it in the music business, and he was equally determined to explore every outlet that would let him make music. Although he was not always successful—his recording was never released, and very few people listened to his broadcast—he was becoming familiar with the many aspects of the musical world. He was learning the business.

four years. Working with the same band members each night helped Ellington grow as a musician.

During those four years, the band experienced two major changes. First, the name was changed to the Washingtonians. Second—and more important—Ellington became the band's leader, and they were playing his music.

The Washingtonians did well for themselves. They began to make regular broadcasts on radio station WHN, and articles about the group were soon appearing in newspapers. One of the reasons for the success of the band was that James "Bubber" Miley replaced Whetsol as a trumpet player. Four years younger than Ellington, Miley originally came from the South. He moved to New York in 1923 when he met Ellington—and quickly became well known for his natural talent plus the distinctive "wah wah" sound he produced on his trumpet. His style of playing the instrument attracted a lot of attention and gave the band a special sound.

Ellington was still attempting to get his songs published. In the fall of 1923, he and lyricist Jo Trent were able to sell "Blind Man's Buff," although the song was never published.

At this time, Ellington became friends with Will Marion Cook, a highly trained African-American composer and conductor. Cook had studied music at some of the country's most respected conservatories, including Oberlin

The Washingtonians in the early 1920s. Ellington is at the left.

and the National Conservatory of Music, which was founded in 1885 and accepted students of all races.

Once again, Ellington learned from a skilled musician by listening and watching. He and Cook would ride in a taxi together around Central Park. As they rode, Cook lectured Ellington about music, giving Ellington plenty of technical advice. He also insisted that the only way Ellington would come into his own as a musician was by being himself and following his own musical instincts.

Ellington continued to grow musically, and so did the band. The Washingtonians had added a job performing at the Cinderella Ballroom, where they played before appearing at the Hollywood Club. Charlie Irvis, a trombone player known for performing blues, had joined the Washingtonians when Elmer Snowden, the band's former leader, left. It was easy for Ellington to slip into the role of bandleader. It was a position he would hold for the rest of his life.

The Washingtonians traveled to Massachusetts during 1924, playing in Boston as well as smaller cities. Ellington also made several recordings that year. Three of them were songs he had written.

When a fire damaged the Hollywood Club in 1925, Ellington's orchestra traveled back to Massachusetts to perform at dances. The Hollywood Club, renamed the Kentucky Club, opened its doors again later that year. The Washingtonians played dance music at the club for several hours each evening until midnight and then accompanied singers or other acts at midnight and again at two in the morning.

Ellington said, "Late at night we'd send the band home and Sonny Greer and I would work the floor, take one of those little pianos and push it around the floor from party to party."[4]

The group had grown to include a tuba player, Henry "Bass" Edwards. Although most of the musicians left the Kentucky Club after their final midnight performance, Ellington and Greer continued playing. Their music drew large audiences, and the dance floor became so crowded it was often impossible to find room to dance. The club remained open until seven in the morning, and the musicians worked hard, earning large tips for their efforts.

The Washingtonians drew big crowds of appreciative listeners. The band also attracted the attention of Tommy Dorsey, a jazz trombonist who would eventually become famous when he formed his own band. Ellington's band stood out from similar groups at that time because the musicians were encouraged to play their own arrangements of standard pieces. When the band played a popular song of the day, Ellington's musicians gave the piece its own special sound.

Ellington and Jo Trent were still working together on songs. In the spring of 1925, the men were asked to write a show called *Chocolate Kiddies*. The only problem was that they had to come up with the songs before the next day. "Being dumb, and not knowing any better, I sat down that evening and wrote a show," Ellington said.[5]

Never willing to back down from a challenge or hard work, Ellington and Trent came up with songs for the show, which included "Jim Dandy," "Jig Walk," "With You," and "Love Is Just a Wish for You." The promoter, Jack Robbins, who would later head the major music publishing house of Robbins Music, liked the songs but was not able to get the show staged in New York. It did, however, open in Berlin, Germany, and then toured through Europe and Russia under the title *Negro Operetta*. Ellington was given five hundred dollars for his work, comparable to more than five thousand dollars today.

Before long, the band was called Duke Ellington and His Washingtonians. Joe "Tricky Sam" Nanton took the place of the trombone player Charlie Irvis. Just as Ellington had been drawn to Miley's original sound on the trumpet, he now chose Nanton for his personal style on the trombone. It was one of Ellington's special gifts that he could find musicians who fit in well with the band and then developed their own special style of playing.

The Kentucky Club was forced to close in the summer of 1926. So Ellington and his band traveled to New England, where they performed at dances throughout the area. Dance halls were very popular in the 1920s, and

By the end of the 1920s, Duke Ellington
was ready to take on the world.

◆◆◆◆◆

many Americans flocked to public ballrooms to enjoy what had become a national pastime.

By this time, Ellington's band was very successful. He worked hard to keep it that way, attending to even the smallest details himself. Ellington knew that the band's appearance was important for its overall image. He wanted audiences and critics to think highly of his musicians. He made sure that everyone dressed well—including himself. In the course of a day, Ellington often changed his own clothes several times. During his lifetime, he kept more than 150 suits in his closets and more than 1,000 ties.

Ellington still wanted more. He wanted to be the best. He knew that a larger audience needed to hear his band play. One day Ellington met Irving Mills, who owned a music publishing company and also made recordings. Mills wanted to record the Washingtonians, and Ellington readily agreed. By 1928, Ellington had made a deal with Mills. They formed a corporation in which Ellington had 45 percent ownership.

Mills believed that the Washingtonians' best work came out of the pieces Ellington had written. He was interested in recording Ellington's compositions rather than standard pieces of the day. Ellington made his first recording with Mills in late

> Mills believed that the Washingtonians' best work came out of the pieces Ellington had written.

November 1926. For the record label, the band was called Duke Ellington and His Kentucky Club Orchestra. Two of the pieces they recorded were Ellington's "East St. Louis Toodle-Oo" and "Birmingham Breakdown."

"East St. Louis Toodle-Oo" is considered a masterpiece by most music critics, and the piece was successful from the start. Ellington began recording music with several companies, while Irving Mills published the written compositions. The year Ellington turned twenty-eight, he made thirty-one recordings, including the popular "Black and Tan Fantasy" and "Creole Love Call." Through hard work, Ellington was bringing his music to more and more listeners. He wanted his name to get around—and he was making it happen.

Chapter 5

The Cotton Club

llington's days were filled with making his band the best. He rehearsed the musicians in the afternoon, played at dances and nightclubs in the evening, and used his off hours to work on compositions.

"I've always preferred to mix dances and concerts, to play highbrow stuff in the concert hall . . . and the next night to play a prom. . . . I like the change of pace in going from one extreme to the another. We have so much stuff in the book, and not only jazz," he said.[1]

Ellington's music was inspired by Harlem, and his songs reflected the lives of average African Americans. He read a lot about black history and owned hundreds of books on the topic.

"I am just getting a chance to work out some of my own ideas of Negro music," he said. "I stick to that. We as a race have a good deal to pay our way with in a white world. The tragedy is that so few records have been kept of the Negro music of the past. It has to be pieced together so slowly. But it pleases me to have a chance to work at it."[2]

The band toured New England in the summer of 1927 and returned to New York by September. Their contract had run out with the Kentucky Club that previous spring, so the musicians performed at Club Ciro's and in theatrical entertainments called revues. A revue is a kind of variety show that combines music, dancing, and short skits. At the Lafayette Theater, the band played in *Jazzmania* and *Dance Mania* to excellent critical reviews. They performed in a show called *Messin' Around* at the Plantation Club.

By this time, a few new members had joined Ellington's band. Rudy Jackson, who originally came from Chicago, played clarinet. Wellman Braud played bass and Harry Carney, only seventeen, played both clarinet and saxophone.

With his recordings and a collection of talented musicians, Ellington seemed to have everything in place. All he needed now was somewhere the band could perform on a regular basis. That place turned out to be the Cotton Club in Harlem.

The Cotton Club opened its doors as the Club Deluxe in 1920 during Prohibition. The heavyweight African-American boxing champion Jack Johnson was the original owner. The club was taken over a couple of years later by

Owney Madden, a white gangster and a bootlegger—that is, a person who sold alcohol illegally during Prohibition. Madden changed the club's name to the Cotton Club. The police closed the club in 1925 for selling liquor, but before long it was back in business without any further trouble.

The band that had been performing there each night was Andy Preer's Cotton Club Syncopators. After Preer died in 1927, Ellington took his band to the club to audition. The Washingtonians showed up late, and several other bands had already played. Luckily, one of the Cotton Club's managers was also late, so he had not heard any of the other bands. After listening to Ellington's musicians, he hired them right away.

Ellington's band, however, had already agreed to travel to Philadelphia with *Dance Mania*. How could they back out of a job they had been hired to do? The Cotton Club had some connections with gangsters, and these men visited the Philadelphia theater where the Washingtonians were to perform. "Be big or you'll be dead," one gangster told the theater people in Philadelphia.[3] His words meant: Let the band out of its agreement.

They chose "big," and Ellington's musicians left Philadelphia and headed to the Cotton Club.

Although the musicians and employees were black, the customers at the Cotton Club were white. The audiences that appeared at the club each night came from the top level of New York's social circle. The best jazz musicians of

The Cotton Club had a reputation for great music, but it also had shady owners that were connected to organized crime.

the day performed there, and the club was the most famous of New York's nightclubs during the early 1900s.

The Washingtonians played their first performance at the Cotton Club on December 4, 1927. Over the next four years, the band would appear at the club, with its musicians considered among the best in the country. Yet their first few performances at the club did not go smoothly.

One problem was that Ellington liked choosing his own musicians. He looked for musicians he thought would blend in well with the rest of the orchestra, as well as those who had a special sound to bring to the group. But in those early days at the Cotton Club, Ellington had to deal with some temporary musicians. He also had to play many songs that were not his choice. The singers and dancers at the club were allowed to select certain pieces and the group was not used to playing music that was written by

African-American Pride

Ellington's parents had raised him to be proud of his African-American heritage. While he may have been unhappy that the Cotton Club served only white customers, he was a businessman above all—and a very ambitious one. He knew that appearing regularly at the club would put his band in the national spotlight. Throughout his life, Ellington would be accused of not taking a strong stand when African Americans were treated unfairly.

"People who think that of me," he said, "haven't been listening to our music. For a long time, social protest and pride of the Negro have been the most significant things in what we've done."[4]

other composers. In addition to all this, Ellington was used to spending many hours rehearsing his musicians to get exactly the sound he wanted. The fact that the band had been hired quickly—and pulled away from the revue in Philadelphia—left him with little time to prepare these new songs and work with the new musicians. "We were established and we were doing so well, but the pressure went on," said Greer:

> We had to enlarge the band, too and that broke my heart, because everything had been so quiet and tasteful. We hadn't had written arrangements. We'd just talk things over and make suggestions on the interpretation. . . . The way he blended his band, our 6 or 7 sounded like 12 pieces.[5]

Ellington's band did not play on the stage, but was part of the entire theater experience. Ellington had already spent much of his life observing how audiences responded to different musicians. Listening and watching carefully, he had studied how to put on a good show. Now he was doing just that, and it did not take long for the band to feel comfortable in its new home. Although the gangsters who ran the club did not care for Ellington's music at first, they did like the fact that business picked up with the arrival of Ellington's band. Even the customers and critics who in the beginning did not like the music quickly changed their minds.

The theme of the Cotton Club was both southern and African, and Ellington's music was supposed to reflect those themes. With this in mind, he wrote such pieces as

"Jungle Blues," "Jungle Jamboree," "Jungle Nights in Harlem," and "Hottentot." The music Ellington needed to compose was different, and he had fun with it, writing in parts for specific instruments to give the music an exotic flavor. Combined with the stage shows, which featured energetic dancers in unusual costumes, the performances

Ellington (center) and his band pose for a publicity shot for the Cotton Club.

drew more and more people to the Cotton Club each night. The final show at the Cotton Club went on at two in the morning, and its doors finally closed at four o'clock. "Then everybody would go next door to Happy Roane's or to the breakfast dance at Smalls' Paradise, where the floor-show went on at six o'clock in the morning," said Greer. "The average musician hated to go home in those days. He was always seeking some place where someone was playing something he ought to hear. Ten o'clock in the morning, someone would come by and say, 'Man, they're jamming at so-and-so's,' and over he'd go."[6]

Working at the Cotton Club did more for Ellington's career than just putting his band in the spotlight. It gave him the chance to develop his style of composing. Having to write a completely new show twice a year forced him to become more creative and experiment with different kinds of music.

As always, the orchestra was undergoing changes. Instead of Rudy Jackson on clarinet, Ellington hired Barney Bigard, who was able to make his clarinet heard above the brass while holding onto a strong sound. Johnny Hodges came on as the alto sax player and became one of the band's most famous soloists. Hodges was self-taught for the most part, and he produced a clear, pure tone in both blues songs and ballads.

When Ellington played at the Cotton Club, radio stations broadcast the performance. His music was reaching an audience far beyond the club's walls. Now called Duke Ellington and His Cotton Club Orchestra, the band's unique sound entered the homes of Americans as they ate dinner or enjoyed the radio in the evening hours.

In the spring of 1928, Ellington wrote such songs as "Hot and Bothered," "The Mooche," and "Swampy River," a piano solo. In the fall, his musical compositions won him excellent reviews from the New York critics. It seemed as if customers were now flocking to the Cotton Club just to hear Ellington's band.

> It seemed as if customers were now flocking to the Cotton Club just to hear Ellington's band.

At the start of 1929, Ellington replaced James Miley, one of his trumpet players, with Charles Williams, a teenager known as "Cootie." Originally from Alabama, Williams had taught himself how to play the trumpet. He had already toured with several bands before moving to New York in 1928. Williams quickly learned the kind of jungle growl Ellington wanted him to produce. Excellent at improvising—performing on the spot with little or no preparation—Williams brought his own special sound to the band.

"In the beginning, you didn't think about money," said Williams. "It was exciting, and we were very young.

Everybody made suggestions. It was a family thing."[7] He would remain with Ellington for more than twenty years.

Ellington continued performing and making recordings. He also made a movie for RKO film studio in 1929. This short movie, less than twenty minutes, was titled *Black and Tan*. One plotline focused on a jazz bandleader—played by Ellington—who falls in love with a dancer. Ellington would appear in many more movies throughout his life, yet this was one of the few times he would be hired as an actor as well as a musician.

Shortly after Ellington's appearance in *Black and Tan*, he and his band were asked to perform in the Ziegfeld Follies. Managed by Florenz Ziegfeld, the Follies were a kind of high-class variety show. They were very popular in the early 1900s and helped pave the way for today's Broadway musicals. Ellington was to perform in *Show Girl*, playing music written by George Gershwin. The composer Gershwin became famous during his short life for popular songs, as well as classical music in which he often blended in elements of jazz. The show featured one of Gershwin's most famous works, "An American in Paris." The performers included some top stars of the day: Jimmy Durante, Al Jolson, and Ruby Keeler. Ellington's band sat on stage and played in several pieces. They did this each night for more than one hundred performances. One night, Ellington's former piano teacher, Mrs. Clinkscales, sat in the audience.

Soon Ellington had a whole orchestra to play with at the Cotton Club.

Afterward, the musicians headed over to the Cotton Club, where they performed at midnight and again at two in the morning. The lifestyle was hectic, but it seemed to suit Ellington. "After he performed, he'd be wide awake and energized," said Patricia Willard, Ellington's press agent. "He'd stay up all night writing and would get drowsy about 9 A.M. Nobody could ever get him during normal business hours. Everybody who was close to him just got used to it."[8]

Ellington was always in motion. "I can remember nights when Ellington would come home, say around 3:30, and I'd been asleep already," said his son, Mercer. "I'd hear these strains being played on the piano—almost in my sleep. . . . Those, I think, were really my first lessons in composition."[9]

If Ellington always kept busy, he also was always late. It was his personality to do things at the last minute, and he hated being asked to hurry. Usually, a few members of the band stayed close to Ellington when they were getting ready to put on a show. They had to make sure he would show up on time for the performance.

With regular appearances at the Cotton Club and his orchestra in demand elsewhere, Ellington was making more money than he had ever earned before. He was becoming known throughout the United States as the leader of a first-class band.

Chapter 6

New Horizons

The Great Depression, which began in 1929, had a direct effect on the entertainment industry. People looked to movies, music, and dancing to take their minds off their troubles. Musical films and comedies helped people forget the hard times—if only for a couple of hours. Big bands, with their lively up-beat sound, drew large crowds as they played swing music.

The thirty-year-old Ellington continued performing and recording. He made records with all the big companies in 1929 and 1930. Each company gave the orchestra a different name, so that it seemed as if Ellington's band recorded only for that label. For example, on the Brunswick label Ellington's musicians were called the Jungle Band, while on the OKeh label they were listed as the Harlem Footwarmers.

The Great Depression

In October 1929, many Americans who had invested money in the stock market suddenly found themselves penniless. The stock market crash forced banks to close, and the country was plunged into an economic depression. The Great Depression lasted until the mid 1930s. There were few jobs, and many people did not have enough to eat. Businessmen who had once been millionaires were now selling pencils on street corners. One third of all Americans were living in poverty.

By late 1929, Ellington's orchestra was made up of twelve members. He had added a second trombone player, and with all the brass instruments, the group had a very full sound. Ellington continued writing and performing revues for the Cotton Club.

His sister, Ruth, said that Ellington would come home from the Cotton Club around three or four in the morning. "I would be going to High School," she said, "and sleeping in the room right next to him he would be playing the piano softly all night long."[1]

In March 1930, the orchestra appeared in concert for two weeks with the famous French singer Maurice Chevalier. He had been a star of musical comedies on stage and in the movies ever since his first musical, at age thirteen.

Ellington's band was not used to performing in a concert where the audience focused its full attention on the music. Typically, Ellington and his musicians provided background music to the main act on stage. For all his experience and confidence, Ellington was nervous when he had to stand on stage as master of ceremonies and speak to the audience. The Cotton Club had an announcer, but in the concert engagement with Chevalier, Ellington was on his own. It would be many years before he felt comfortable talking directly to an audience.

While performing at the Cotton Club, the band accepted other engagements—a revue at the Lafayette Theater in Harlem and a two-week gig at the very popular Palace Theater. The musicians then took a brief break from the Cotton Club and traveled to Baltimore, Boston, Chicago, Detroit, and Pittsburgh, performing in ballrooms, where public dancing continued to rank as one of the main forms of entertainment.

Irving Mills, with whom Ellington had formed a partnership several years earlier, was working hard to promote Ellington's orchestra. He arranged a tour of several cities from Baltimore to Chicago and also landed the band a spot in a Hollywood film, *Check and Double Check*. It marked Ellington's first appearance in a feature-length film.

The movie starred two white comedians who played black characters named Amos 'n' Andy on a popular radio show. Amos Jones was played by Freeman Gosden, and the role of Andy Brown was handled by Charles Correll. Gosden and Correll traveled to Hollywood in 1930 to play Amos 'n' Andy in *Check and Double Check*. The two actors appeared in blackface, that is, they made themselves up to look like African Americans. It is considered racist today when whites appear in blackface.

At that time, many people did not believe blacks and whites should be allowed to mix socially or at work. The movie-studio executives wanted to be sure that audiences knew that Ellington's musicians were African American, that blacks and whites were not playing in the same orchestra. So they told two of the lighter-skinned men that they must play in blackface. The band was paid $5,000 a week and performed such songs in the film as "East St. Louis Toodle-Oo," "Ring Dem Bells," and "Old Man Blues."

By the late 1920s, Mercer Ellington was living with his parents in New York. The Ellingtons' marriage, however, was not doing well. The couple argued heatedly when they were together. During one fight, Edna struck her husband's cheek with a knife. Ellington would bear the scar for the rest of his life. They finally separated, though they never divorced. Throughout the 1930s, Ellington lived with Mildred Dixon, a dancer at the Cotton Club. When Ellington bought an expensive apartment in the nicest section of Harlem, he moved in with Mildred, Mercer, his sister, and his parents.

Because the country was still going through hard economic times, many musicians found themselves out of work. Orchestras, which cost a lot of money to hire because of the large number of musicians, were often replaced by less expensive solo performers. Few people could afford to buy records. More and more Americans got through these hard times by going to the movies or listening to their radios.

The popularity of Ellington's orchestra grew as a result of these radio broadcasts. Nearly every night of the week, the Cotton Club broadcast Ellington's band around eleven o'clock on CBS radio. It was the only African-American orchestra the station carried. Soon Ellington also had a regular spot on NBC radio, one of the country's major networks. The orchestra was broadcast on Saturday nights between eleven and midnight. Ellington began writing music especially for these radio broadcasts. Often, listeners would

Early radios were almost like furniture in the 1930s. Families would gather around them to listen to programs like comedy shows or music like Duke Ellington and his orchestra.

write to the stations praising the songs they had heard. One such piece, "Mood Indigo," became one of Ellington's most popular and most critically acclaimed compositions ever.

As 1930 drew to a close, Ellington's orchestra became the first African-American group to perform at the Paramount Theater on Broadway. Mills now believed it was time for the band to go on a tour throughout the country. The group took a break from its steady nightly performances at the Cotton Club and went on the road in February 1931.

Ellington had worked hard to bring his name into American homes. In jazz circles, he was as popular as Louis Armstrong, the trumpeter from New Orleans who was also known as "Satchmo." Ellington's orchestra had made close to two hundred recordings over the past four years. The band had also appeared in movies, had performed live at the Cotton Club, and was being broadcast regularly on the radio. The orchestra's popularity continued to grow as it toured the country in the early 1930s.

The musicians traveled from city to city, performing in locations that included Boston, Chicago, Minneapolis, St. Louis, and Cincinnati. They stayed in each city for about a week before moving on to the next. The daily schedule was jam-packed, but Ellington was used to this lifestyle.

MOOD INDIGO
by Duke Ellington, Irving Mills & Albany Bigard

"Mood Indigo" became a very popular piece for Ellington.

While on tour, Ellington added a female singer to the group. Twenty-five-year-old Ivie Anderson was able to connect with the audience with her sensitive singing style and easy sense of rhythm. Her voice was sweet and clear and she was a welcome addition to the orchestra. At Chicago's Oriental Theater, Anderson was called back after her performances to take four bows and even then had to make a speech before the audience would allow her to leave the stage. She would end up staying with the group for eleven years.

The management at the Oriental Theater asked Ellington's orchestra to perform five times during 1931. Each time, the theater was packed and Ellington's performances brought in more money than the theater had ever pulled in before.

Part of the appeal of Ellington's music was that it blended so many different styles and sounds. "He had to make his own rules because there were no rules for what he was doing," said Wynton Marsalis, a present-day trumpeter and composer. "He drew on New Orleans music, work songs, Tin Pan Alley, Armstrong, spirituals, the minstrel tradition. He made something we could recognize as being about us."[2]

Musically, Ellington's time in Chicago was a success. Personally, however, he ran into some trouble. Ellington was fined $2,000 by the musicians' union for allowing the members of his orchestra to accept less money than the

In 1931, Ellington and his orchestra took the stage
at the Regal Theatre in Chicago.

amount set by the union—$4.92 less per musician. In addition, gangsters in Chicago threatened to kidnap Ellington. But the owner of the Cotton Club, Owney Madden, knew Al Capone, the most notorious gangster in Chicago. Capone arranged for some of his men to show up with guns and tell the other gangsters to stay away from Ellington. After that, Ellington was left alone.

> Gangsters in Chicago threatened to kidnap Ellington.

Ellington, like other African Americans at that time, had to deal with prejudice because of the color of his skin. At times, Ellington's orchestra was not broadcast over national radio because no company would run ads on a show with black performers. In Philadelphia, Ellington's car was broken into and some of his possessions were stolen. It was never determined whether the attack was aimed at Ellington himself or meant to protest his orchestra's playing in a white neighborhood.

In St. Louis, Ellington and his musicians were forced to ride a freight elevator in a hotel because the white man running the regular elevator refused to allow the orchestra members to enter.

Occasionally, Ellington took a definite stand against prejudice. He performed at a concert in Washington that was held to benefit the Scottsboro boys—nine African-American boys who had been convicted of rape by an

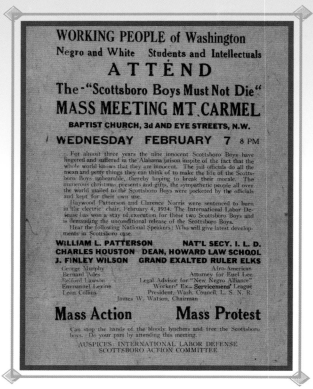

This poster advertises a rally in support of the Scottsboro boys, a cause that Duke Ellington supported.

all-white southern jury without having proper lawyers of their own.

Ellington did not usually speak out against this kind of unfair treatment, although he had always cared deeply about promoting the dignity and respect of African Americans. He believed that he could best help fight prejudice by being a well-spoken, well-mannered, and highly successful black musician and businessman.

Chapter 7

A Temporary Halt

llington's popularity had spread from the United States to Europe. His recordings—especially "Mood Indigo," which Victor Records called its record of the month in February 1931—sold in great numbers throughout England and France, where jazz had a wide audience. Ellington was doing well for himself, earning up to $6,000 a week for performances. Readers of the *Pittsburgh Courier* voted his orchestra the most popular, and the newspaper presented him with a trophy in honor of winning the contest.

Ellington enjoyed having money to spend, and he often spent it on food. He liked eating and was known for his ability to eat enormous quantities of food. For example, he could consume a dinner of two steaks, a lobster with butter, two orders of French fries, a few tomatoes, salad, coffee, and dessert. His desserts were also on the heavy side: three slices of three different cakes, each with a scoop of ice cream on it, and then some kind of topping. Often Ellington was *still* hungry and would then eat waffles, pancakes, ham, eggs, and biscuits. Surprisingly, his weight stayed between 185 and 210 pounds on his six-foot-one-inch frame.

Some musicians would sit back and enjoy the success of leading such a popular band. But not Ellington. As always, he was interested in experimenting with his orchestra's sound. The composer Billy Strayhorn once said, "Ellington plays piano, but his real instrument is his band."[1]

Ellington felt limited by the typical recording, which had only three minutes of playing time on each side. In 1932, he decided to record a medley (several songs combined as a whole unit) of his works. The first medley he recorded included "Mood Indigo," "Hot and Bothered," and "Creole Love Call." Shortly after this, he recorded a second medley, using "East St. Louis Toodle-Oo," "Black and Tan Fantasy," and "Lots o' Fingers." One of his individual songs at that time became hugely popular: "It Don't Mean a Thing (If It Ain't Got That Swing)."

In 1932, Ellington was getting ready to hire another trombone player. Lawrence Brown, a highly talented musician, would add to the band's full, rich sound.

The sheet music for "It Don't Mean a Thing" had a modern design and Ellington's picture on the cover.

However, Ellington was a very superstitious man, and he did not want his orchestra to be made up of thirteen musicians—an unlucky number. So Ellington also asked his old friend Toby Hardwick to rejoin the group as saxophonist. Hardwick agreed, bringing the count to a comfortable fourteen.

Ellington enjoyed writing music specifically for these top musicians. "I give them the money, and I get the kicks," he said.[2] Another advantage to being surrounded by outstanding musicians on a day-to-day basis was that Ellington could hear his music performed as soon as he wrote it. This gave him almost instant feedback on his work, and it allowed him to take chances.

The jazz trumpeter Clark Terry said, "Duke had hundreds of different ways of using the blues. He experimented. He was daring enough to try new things. He was the top of the pole: As Duke went, so went jazz."[3]

Ellington's personality was as distinctive as his music. He had various habits and superstitions that were very much his own. He refused to wear the color green. Green reminded him of grass, he said, and grass made him think of graves in a cemetery.

"I heard that he was wearing a brown suit when his mother died, and after that he could never stand the sight of brown," said Patricia Willard. "Anything he associated with success and happy times he would repeat, but anything that reminded him of sadness he would absolutely avoid. His life was not easy, and in order to keep going and creating, I think he had to think positively."[4]

Ellington took numerous vitamins each day and worried a lot about his health. He did not like fresh air, so he always closed the windows when he entered a room. His sleep habits were also unusual. Normally, Ellington did not go to bed until the early hours of the morning. But many times, he did not go to bed at all for several days in a row. When he did sleep, he slept like a rock. One time, he fell asleep on a train ride to California. Although

The Sound of Duke Ellington

Although much of what Ellington's orchestra played was his own music, the group also performed standard dance-band songs such as "Stardust" and "Stormy Weather." But even those pieces were stamped with Ellington's own arrangements. Whatever the Ellington orchestra played came out sounding original.

Ellington's musicians did not use written music during their performances. Ellington did not like the way it looked when musicians stared at printed music while playing their parts. So when he rehearsed the group at night, Ellington would tell each musician what to play by demonstrating on the piano. The musician would imitate Ellington's technique and memorize his part so he could perform the next day without music.

Ellington got off the train at the proper stop, he was still groggy. By accident, he got into a van that was bound for San Quentin prison. Ellington was allowed out of the van only when the mistake was explained to the prison guard.

By this time, Ellington's fame was extending beyond the nightclub and dance-hall scene. In late 1932, the composer and pianist Percy Grainger invited Ellington and his band to perform at New York University (NYU). Grainger, who came from Australia, was the dean of music at the university. As a composer he enjoyed experimenting with new ideas—such as playing the piano by hitting the strings with a mallet instead of striking the keys with his fingers—and he decided to include jazz classes at NYU. Ellington performed with his orchestra in a music appreciation class and was a guest lecturer.

Two months later, Ellington won the New York School of Music's award for best composition of the year. The school officials chose "Creole Rhapsody," with its portrayal of African-American life. New York's mayor, John P. O'Brien, presented the award to Ellington.

Ellington was back at Harlem's Cotton Club in 1933. He performed with such stars of the day as Ethel Merman, Ray Bolger, Eddie Cantor, and Milton Berle. When the summer rolled around, Ellington took his orchestra to Europe for a two month tour. Crossing the Atlantic Ocean was difficult for Ellington because he was afraid of water

Ellington always made sure his musicians were well dressed.

and of being shipwrecked. During the voyage, he stayed up all night, every night, playing cards and drinking.

In spite of the fact that the musicians had a difficult time finding housing because of their skin color, the tour was a musical success. The orchestra played to sell-out crowds, breaking all previous records for ticket sales at

London's Palladium. Ellington made sure the musicians were spotless and well dressed. The polished instruments gleamed. "He said we should play pretty and look pretty," said Greer.[5]

While in England, Ellington became friendly with members of the royal family. He allowed the Prince of Wales to play the drums and the Duke of Kent to share a piano duet with him. The British loved Ellington. When he played for a broadcast on the BBC, the radio station paid Ellington more money than it had ever given an American performer. The British considered Ellington a serious composer, and by the time he left England, approximately one hundred thousand people had heard him and his orchestra play.

In Paris, France, the orchestra was also praised. The French loved jazz, and the musicians were admired whenever they played.

The success of the tour in Europe increased Ellington's popularity back in the United States. He felt encouraged to continue refining and experimenting with his sound.

"Duke thrived [on ideas]," said Greer. "We'd be sitting up playing cards and he'd get an idea, he'd write it down on paper."[6]

Ellington had not wanted his band to tour the southern United States because of how unfairly blacks were treated there. If it had been hard for the musicians to find hotels in England, it was nearly impossible in the South.

African Americans who traveled there generally wound up staying in private homes or in boarding houses. Most restaurants would not serve black customers, so it was difficult finding places to eat.

Yet Irving Mills managed to talk Ellington into making the trip. The first stop was the Majestic Theater in Dallas, Texas. Not only did Ellington's musicians receive rave reviews from the critics, but the theater took in more money than at any time in its history.

The success of his orchestra—and the money that followed that success—allowed Ellington to afford private railroad cars. Travel became easier now that the band had its own baggage car for instruments and sound equipment. There were two sleeper cars for the musicians. With the addition of a private dining car, they could even prepare their own meals while traveling by railroad. These came in particularly handy when the orchestra traveled through the South.

The orchestra performed in Oklahoma, Louisiana, Alabama, Georgia, and Tennessee. "We commanded respect," said Ellington. "We didn't travel by bus. Instead we had two Pullman cars and a 70-foot baggage car. We parked in each station and lived in the Pullman cars. The natives would come by and say, 'What's that?' 'Well,' we'd say, 'that's the way the president travels.'"[7]

There were no racial problems during the tour, yet the audiences were segregated—blacks and whites had to sit in separate sections. Sometimes Ellington would play one performance for whites and another for blacks.

These were creative years for Ellington. He wrote a number of pieces, including "Daybreak Express," "Jive Stomp," "Solitude," and "Blue Feeling." The travel was tiring, but Ellington enjoyed it. The time he spent on trains gave him privacy and a chance to think. "You'd see him in a siding somewhere in Texas, the heat at 110, the sweat pouring off him onto a piece of manuscript paper on his knee, catching up on something he wanted to finish," said his sister, Ruth.[8]

Ellington turned his attention once again to movies. In 1934, the orchestra appeared in *Murder of the Vanities* and *Belle of the Nineties*, both feature length films from Paramount Studios. In *Belle of the Nineties*, the band accompanied actress Mae West in four numbers. West was a popular American actress who was known for her frequent jokes and bold manner of speaking. Early in her career, West wrote her own plays and performed them onstage. But her popularity was based on her many film roles.

That same year, Ellington's orchestra worked in *Symphony in Black: A Rhapsody of Negro Life*. The movie focused on black life in the cotton industry. One of the actresses in the movie was Billie Holiday. Later in her career, Holiday would be considered one of the greatest jazz singers of all time.

Duke Ellington first met Billie Holiday in 1934. Here, Ellington and Holiday review a piece of music along with jazz critic Leonard Feather (right) in 1945.

Tragedy struck Ellington's life when he turned thirty-six: His mother died. Ellington had always been extremely close to Daisy Ellington, and her death hit him hard. For the first time since his teenage years, Ellington did not take an interest in music. The energy seemed to leave him, and he spent a period of time drinking heavily and sinking deeper into his gloom.

"I have no ambition left," he said. "When mother was alive I had something to fight for, I could say, 'I'll fight with anybody, against any kinda odds.' . . . Now what? I can see nothing. The bottom's out of everything."[9]

Ellington had never liked jewelry and did not wear rings or watches. After his mother's death, he started wearing a gold cross around his neck.

He eventually dealt with his grief in the way that seemed most natural for him—he composed a piece of music. "Reminiscing in Tempo," written for his mother, was his most ambitious effort to date. The composition took up four record sides. It was twice as long even as "Creole Rhapsody." Some music reviewers criticized the piece, calling it pretentious.

Ellington did not make any more recordings that year and the four songs he did record in 1936 were not successful. When the man in charge of publicity for Ellington's band stopped working for Irving Mills, Ellington and his orchestra did not get hired as frequently. They often had to play one-night dance engagements. After riding such a huge wave of success for so long, it seemed that Ellington had come temporarily to a halt.

Also at this time, swing music suddenly gripped the nation. Swing was a type of jazz music that featured a strong rhythm section and a quick tempo. Crowds flocked to hear the top swing bands, such as Benny Goodman's group. Goodman, who played clarinet, is often given credit for starting the swing era.

Ellington's music at times ventured into swing, but it was not focused on providing a steady beat for dance. Ellington was always exploring melody and harmony. He was interested in making music, *his* kind of music. He did not like giving the music he played any kind of label. He believed that most swing music had its roots in African-

With a baton in hand, Duke Ellington (top) leads his jazz band.

American music and said that "the Negro has done more to create a distinctively American music than any other race."[10]

While the swing bands grabbed a large share of the audience in the late 1930s, Ellington decided he would continue to make his own kind of music. He wrote some compositions that specifically featured particular musicians, such as "Clarinet Lament" for his clarinetist Barney Bigard and "Echoes of Harlem" for his trumpet player Cootie Williams.

Ellington also worked on several jazz pieces that involved a handful of musicians rather than his entire orchestra. The small-band numbers were recorded on the Variety label. During a two-year period, Ellington made 140 recordings with his small groups. Although these groups were often led by a featured soloist, such as Cootie Williams on the trumpet or Johnny Hodges on the sax, Ellington was still very much in charge. He decided which players would perform in specific songs, and he handled the arrangements of the pieces. Ellington also took his place at the piano for these sessions.

Ellington was aware that the public's taste in music was changing. Yet he was determined to continue writing music that reflected his sound.

Chapter 8

Beyond Barriers

The Cotton Club had been forced to close for a while in 1936. Harlem had erupted in racial riots, and afterward, business had been poor. When it reopened later that year—about a block away from the Kentucky Club—Ellington's orchestra played in a full-scale revue that included the singers George Dewey and Ethel Waters. The band performed there for three months. Once again, the musicians received excellent reviews from the critics.

Now in his mid-thirties, Ellington wrote "Crescendo in Blue" and "Diminuendo in Blue," two longer compositions similar to the piece he wrote after his mother's death. Ellington's father was a heavy drinker and in poor health. In October 1937, James Ellington died. With both his parents gone, Ellington took charge of his sister, Ruth, who was sixteen years younger. Acting as a substitute father,

Ellington and his band in 1937

❖ ❖ ❖ ❖ ❖

Ellington was caring and protective of his twenty-two-year-old sister.

Swing music continued to captivate the nation and to provide competition for the kind of music Ellington's orchestra played. Often, Ellington would compete in battle-of-the-band contests. His musicians always came together to be the best. At one of these contests in 1937, more than three thousand people came to hear Ellington's orchestra compete against Chick Webb's band. The Chick Webb Orchestra was the house band at the Savoy, one of Harlem's largest nightclubs. Because of a childhood illness, Webb did not have much use of his legs. He had taken up the drums when doctors suggested it would help his stiff joints. Not even five feet tall, he used special pedals that were made just for him.

Although in 1937 Ellington did not make as many recordings as in past years, he seemed to make up for lost time in 1938. He recorded his new pieces, "Braggin' in Brass," "Battle of Swing," and "I Let a Song Go Out of My Heart," and he made a new recording of his popular "Black and Tan Fantasy." One of his small group recordings, "Jeep's Blues," was also very successful.

As always, Ellington was a perfectionist about his work. If he wrote a piece he did not like, he would tear it up and flush it down the toilet. "If it's good, I'll remember it," he said. "If it's bad, well, I want to forget it, and I'd prefer that no one catches on to how lousy I can write."[1]

Although Ellington had not gone head-to-head in battles of racial prejudice, he had always taken great pride in being black. He believed that his dignified manner and successful career helped fight racial stereotypes. Over the previous few years, Ellington's orchestra had played many "firsts." They were the first African-American band to perform for a long period at a nightclub in Dallas, Texas.

They were also the first black group to play for a white audience in the Orpheum Theatre in Memphis, Tennessee. As they traveled through the South, however, problems had cropped up.

When Juan Tizol, a trombonist from Puerto Rico, went into a restaurant, he found that the staff would serve him (he was light-skinned), but not the rest of the band. He told the workers, "Well, if you don't serve them, you don't serve me either because I'm with them."[2] The restaurant said the band members could get food in the kitchen. Other times Tizol would get food for everyone and take it to the musicians who were waiting in the bus.

When the National Association for the Advancement of Colored People (NAACP) held its annual ball in New York City in 1939, Ellington's orchestra was featured. The gathering of twelve thousand was the largest crowd ever to hear Ellington's music.

By this time, his audience appeal had extended far beyond black listeners. Both his recordings and his radio broadcasts were very popular among whites. Ellington's music had become so popular, in fact, that thirty-seven radio programs used his pieces as their theme songs— numbers such as "In a Sentimental Mood" or "Mood Indigo."

"Duke Ellington earned his success," said Greer. "He worked at it. . . . He began to express some of his dreams by putting different guys into special showcases. Each guy in the band was an individual artist. No two of them ever played alike, and that applies even today. As a team, they're unbeatable. The backgrounds Duke wrote for individual talents not only showed them off to the best advantage, but also made them feel comfortable."[3]

Ellington made some big changes in the late 1930s. He ended his relationship with Mildred Dixon after falling in love with Beatrice "Evie" Ellis, who modeled dresses at the Cotton Club. They moved in together. His son, Mercer, in high school, and sister, Ruth, in teacher's school were on their own.

Ellington also broke off his partnership with Mills. No one is entirely sure whether Ellington felt Mills was not being honest with him about how much money Ellington was earning, or whether Ellington simply wanted to be completely on his own.

Because he had split with Mills and now needed a new agent, Ellington turned to the William Morris Agency. Since Ellington would not use Mills Music anymore to publish his compositions, he signed a deal with Jack Robbins, the same man who had asked him to write the show *Chocolate Kiddies* nearly fifteen years earlier.

Ellington and his musicians boarded a ship in March 1939 and headed for Europe. The French greeted him warmly and the orchestra played to sell-out crowds in Paris. French music reviewers praised the orchestra and after each concert, the audience would beg for more and more songs to be played. Riding on the success of their French tour, the musicians next traveled to Belgium and then on to the Netherlands.

However, the timing of this tour was not the best. The year 1939 was a troubled one for much of Europe. Adolf Hitler, the leader of Germany, planned to expand his empire by invading the European countries around him. There was a feeling of great unrest in Europe.

The band was not slated to perform in Germany, yet they needed to take a train through Germany to get to Denmark and Sweden. There were problems on the train and the orchestra spent a nervous six hours in Germany surrounded by Hitler's soldiers before they could continue their travels.

In Sweden and Norway, the orchestra met with tremendous success. Yet it had become impossible to ignore the situation in Europe. In May, the musicians sailed home where five hundred fans met them at the New York harbor. Four months later, Hitler would lead Germany in an invasion of Poland, triggering the onset of World War II.

Once he was back in New York, Ellington kept a promise to meet with a young musician named Billy Strayhorn.

Almost instantly, Ellington and Strayhorn formed a close partnership. "Sometimes they wouldn't even speak," said press agent Patricia Willard. "Just being in the room, they could communicate with one another."[4]

A Young Musician

Billy Strayhorn

Billy Strayhorn was a composer and pianist who had heard Ellington's orchestra play in Pittsburgh in 1938. Only in his mid-twenties, Strayhorn approached Ellington after the show and explained how he would have arranged one of Ellington's compositions. The band leader was always eager to learn—even if it was from a younger and much less experienced musician. He was impressed with Strayhorn and called over other band members to hear his version of the Ellington piece. Ellington was preparing to take the orchestra on its European tour, but he asked Strayhorn to meet with him as soon as the band returned. While the orchestra traveled through Europe, Strayhorn studied Ellington's music with the help of Ellington's son, Mercer. In this way, Strayhorn learned how to come up with the kind of sound the celebrated bandleader liked.

Strayhorn had studied at the Pittsburgh Music Institute and brought a classically trained ear to Ellington's work. " . . . Any time I was in the throes of debate with myself, harmonically or melodically, I would turn to Billy Strayhorn," Ellington said. "We would talk, and then the whole world would come into focus. The steady hand of his good judgment pointed to the clear way that was most fitting for us."[5]

Strayhorn went on to write lyrics, orchestrations, and pieces of his own, including "Take the A Train," "After All," and "Lotus Blossom."

By the year 1940, the Ellington orchestra was heading once again into a successful and productive time. Ellington had been the band's sole composer before. Now, Strayhorn's original songs relieved him of some of the pressure.

"The kind of things that provide inspiration are always those that nobody . . . ever considers," said Strayhorn. "The public always considers that people who are inspired go off in a fine frenzy, tear their hair and all that business, and then come up with the *Fifth Symphony*. Actually, inspiration comes from the simplest kind of thing, like watching a bird fly. . . . Then the work begins."[6]

For Ellington, it seemed as if inspiration could even come from one of his musicians warming up.

"Cootie used to warm up with the melody that became 'Do Nothing Till You Hear From Me,'" said trumpeter

Ellington and Strayhorn work together on composing a piece of music.

Clark Terry. "Duke heard him do that consistently and made a tune out of it. Cootie would have never composed that thing . . . Duke was a compiler of ideas. He knew how to take insignificant little things and make something out of them."[7]

One of the first performances the William Morris Agency landed for Ellington's band was the 1939 World's Fair held in Flushing, New York City. It was one of the largest fairs that had ever been held, with more than 25 million people attending the exhibits. A main attraction at the fair was one of the first televisions. In addition to performing at the World's Fair, the orchestra also toured different theaters and ballrooms along the East Coast and in the Midwest. "He never accepted the obvious, just because that was the way that was done," said Bob Udkoff, a friend of Ellington's:

> As an example there, at one time we were at his tailor's in Chicago, and he was looking at some materials and said, 'This looks nice,' and the tailor said, 'You're looking at the wrong side, the other side is the right side, that's the back of it!' he said, 'Who says? Why? I like this side.' That was his nature, just because that was the way it was done . . . He didn't follow a leader, he followed what he thought was right.[8]

For a short time, Mercer—who played sax and trumpet—came into his father's band, both arranging and composing music. Some pieces he composed in the early 1940s were "Things Ain't What They Used to Be," "Moon Mist," and

"Blue Serge." Mercer had to leave the band when he was drafted into the army in 1943. By then, the U.S. had been drawn into World War II by the Japanese, who attacked the U.S. Naval base at Pearl Harbor, Hawaii.

There were other changes in the orchestra, such as when Ellington added a fourth trumpet player, Shorty Baker. Although there was turnover within in his band, for the most part, Ellington's musicians liked playing in his band and were loyal to him. They mixed in fun with their hard work. Sometimes they would put itching powder in each other's uniforms or set off a stink bomb on stage. Once, when a violinist was making a guest appearance, the band members put soap on his bow so it would not make any sound when he pulled it across the strings. Another time, they even poured water into the bell of a tuba.

Ellington had always taken care of the business side of his career as carefully as he attended to the musical side. He usually gave his musicians gifts or extra money at the end of the year. He also made sure their travel arrangements were comfortable, he offered opportunities for his musicians to take solo spots, and worked hard to see to it that they had a lot of performances.

"Duke is a great guy to work for," said Ben Webster, a sax player. "He understands musicians better than any leader."[9]

When Cootie Williams, the trumpet player, received an excellent offer to join Benny Goodman's band, he was tempted to take it. Williams had played with Ellington for eleven years and was upset when he told Ellington about the job offer. But Ellington was a practical man and although he would miss Williams, he told him he should accept the higher salary. In fact, Ellington helped Williams work out the deal with Goodman.

Ellington replaced Williams with thirty-six-year-old Ray Nance. An excellent trumpet player, Nance was nicknamed "Floorshow" because he also performed on the violin and sang and danced. One weekend, during a jam session at the home of songwriter Sid Kuller, the idea began to take shape.

> Ellington had been toying with the idea of writing a musical.

"I didn't get in until one in the morning," said Kuller. "The place was swinging. Duke was at the piano, Sonny Greer was at the drums [others, too]. I walked in, 'The joint sure is jumpin'.' Duke turned and said, 'Jumpin' for joy.' I said, 'That's it, why don't we do a show with Ellington, *Jump for Joy*?'"[10]

Ellington composed *Jump for Joy*, which opened in July 1941 at the Mayan Theater in Los Angeles. It was a musical for and about African Americans, with an underlying theme of getting rid of the stereotypes white Americans had about black people.

"We had twelve weeks of discussions after the show [finished each night] concerning the Negro, the race, what constituted Uncle Tom," Ellington said.[11] Uncle Tom is a negative term used for a black person who acts in a servant-like manner toward white people. The show lasted for more than one hundred performances.

One of the songs, "I Got It Bad (and That Ain't Good)," was a hit and the show was praised by just about every music critic. It provided such a positive portrait of black Americans that a review in the *Los Angeles Tribune* read "In *Jump for Joy*, Uncle Tom is dead. God rest his bones."[12]

Ellington's orchestra appeared in 1943 in the movie *Cabin in the Sky*, with such famous stars as trumpeter Louis Armstrong and Lena Horne. Horne was a popular singer who was best known for her work with jazz musicians. Ellington's musicians performed "Things Ain't What They Used to Be" by Mercer, and Ellington's own "Goin' Up." For his contribution to the movie, Ellington earned close to $8,000.

For a long time, Ellington had wanted to write a composition that traced the history of the black race. He worked on the piece and decided to perform it when his orchestra was set to play its first ever performance at Carnegie Hall in New York City. The concert was held on January 23, 1943, and the audience included such famous names as First Lady Eleanor Roosevelt and Leopold Stokowski, the well-known conductor and composer. The concert itself lasted three hours. Close to a third of that was Ellington's new piece "Black, Brown and Beige: A

The movie *Cabin in the Sky* featured Duke Ellington and his orchestra.

Tone Parallel to the History of the Negro in America."
The composition is considered a tone poem, an orchestral
piece that incorporates elements of a poem, novel, or
painting as its theme. Ellington's composition traced the
life of an African man named Boola. It followed his work
experiences, his life as a slave, and his constant efforts to
obtain freedom.

"All through the years, Duke has been deeply concerned about his race and its problems," said Greer. "The feelings of the Negro . . . are there in the music . . . He just composes works like 'Black, Brown and Beige,' *Deep South Suite, Harlem*—leaving it to the people to find and interpret his thoughts for themselves."[13]

The piece did not receive very good reviews, and there were criticisms that it was corny and seemed to be made up of many different parts that did not mesh together into one unit. Ellington performed it only one more time—a few days later—in Boston and then never again.

Chapter 9

Changing
Times

y 1943, Duke Ellington was regarded as one of the country's top bandleaders. This meant he was also one of the best paid. After performing sold-out concerts at Carnegie Hall, Boston's Symphony Hall, and the Civic Auditorium in Cleveland, Ellington's orchestra took a six-week job at the New York nightclub The Hurricane. Six weeks stretched into six months, and it was not until the end of 1943 that Ellington moved on to the Capitol Theater, where he was paid a salary of more than $8,000 a week. The following year, he would receive up to $2,260 for a one-night performance at a dance hall.

Although Ellington was earning large sums of money, he was not terribly wealthy. His expenses were enormous, especially since he had to pay the salaries of as many as thirty people each week. Plus, Ellington was not the kind of person who carefully watched his money. He spent freely; he liked to enjoy himself and that meant good food, fine clothing, massages, and other luxuries. He also gave money to friends who needed help out of their financial difficulties. He lent them money even though they rarely paid him back.

By this time, Ellington owned his own music publishing firm—Tempo Music Company. Very few black composers ran their own publishing firms. It was a bold move for Ellington, and one that showed how much he cared about being totally in charge of his career.

Ellington never became as popular a songwriter as he had hoped. His orchestra was very well known, but for the most part, his songs did not attract the strong following he would have liked. Possibly, this is because he originally wrote many of his songs as instrumental works. He would add the words later. This did not result in the perfect blend of words and lyrics that many songs achieve. In spite of this, Ellington did have three very successful songs in 1943 and 1944: "Don't Get Around Much Anymore," "Do Nothin' Till You Hear from Me," and "I'm Beginning to See the Light."

The country was gripped by World War II once the United States entered it in 1941. Many of Ellington's musicians, including his son Mercer were drafted into the armed forces. Ellington, however, who was in his forties, did not have to take the physical examination that would determine whether or not he was fit to serve in the army. In December 1942, the government had ruled that men older than thirty-eight would not be eligible for the draft.

Throughout the 1940s, Ellington was regularly taking top honors in reader polls held by well-known magazines. Readers of *Down Beat* voted the band as number one among swing bands, and Ellington also was voted best bandleader and arranger by *Esquire* magazine readers. The New York Newspaper Guild honored Ellington with a Page One Award in 1943 and asked him to give a presentation on African-American music at Harvard University. Across the country, there were seventy-five Duke Ellington fan clubs, and a biography was published about his life in 1946, although he was more annoyed than pleased by this. He felt he was too young for a biography; it made it seem as if his career were over.

Ellington's concert at Carnegie Hall had been such a success that by 1948 he played six concerts there. Years earlier, concerts had made Ellington nervous. Now the bandleader enjoyed concert performances because this meant the attention of the audience was devoted solely to the music. In 1946, Ellington was listed as playing the "first real jazz concert" in St. Louis.[1]

When Ellington turned fifty in 1949, he celebrated by appearing on television for the first time. Yet the show *Adventures in Jazz* received a harsh review in *Down Beat*

◆◆◆◆◆◆◆◆◆◆◆◆◆◆◆◆◆◆◆◆◆◆◆◆◆

Doing His Share

Ellington did his part for the war effort by performing at concerts to help war relief efforts in Russia and he also played for the Joint Anti-Fascist Refugee Committee. Ellington's orchestra traveled to different military bases where the musicians played for soldiers. Ellington also recorded programs for the Armed Forces Radio Service and took part in close to fifty shows that were broadcast on network radio as *Your Saturday Date with the Duke*. These shows were intended to help sell war bonds, which raised money for the war effort.

magazine. Writer Mike Levin said the band was "dreary and tired" and played "badly."[2]

At this time, Ellington was having some trouble with his career. For one thing, public interest was turning away from the ballroom scene and the music that had once been so popular in nightclubs. Also, ever since he had lost musicians to the armed forces, Ellington had trouble keeping a regular set of musicians in his band. Turnover was high and this made it harder to produce a consistently tight sound.

To try to bring the orchestra out of this slump, Ellington decided to take the band on a tour of Europe, where his music had always been so well received. The orchestra took two and a half months in the spring of 1950 to travel through France, Belgium, Holland, Switzerland, Italy, Denmark, Sweden, and West Germany. The group played seventy-four concerts.

As always, Ellington kept working on new ideas. Drummer Louis Bellson sat next to Ellington on an airplane and watched Ellington write music on his expensive shirt sleeve because he did not have any paper. "He said if you don't write 'em down you lose 'em," Bellson said.[3]

By the time Ellington returned to the United States, he had put together a composition called "Harlem." The famous conductor Arturo Toscanini had commissioned the fourteen-minute piece and it was recorded in 1951 with the NBC Symphony Orchestra. When Ellington was invited to the White House to meet with President Harry S Truman, he gave the president a copy of the composition.

Ellington performed "Harlem" at a benefit concert for the NAACP in the Metropolitan Opera House in early 1951. Yet his joy at performing at the opera house did not last long. Soon after, three of his top musicians—Johnny Hodges, Sonny Greer, and Lawrence Brown—told Ellington that they were leaving the orchestra to form their own band. Hodges had been Ellington's top soloist and had helped create the Ellington sound. The three musicians had been planning to break away for a while. They had chosen new band uniforms and decided on a name: Johnny Hodges and His Orchestra.

The November 4, 1946 cover of *Down Beat* magazine featured Duke Ellington and his band.

Many music fans wondered if losing three of his top players would force Ellington to retire. But that was not Ellington's way. He hired musicians to replace those who left. One was trombone player Juan Tizol, who had played with him years ago. Tizol had been playing with a band led by Harry James, a well-known trumpet player who had formed his own big band in 1939. Ellington also took James' drummer, Louis Bellson, and his alto sax player, Willie Smith. Ellington found some other musicians, including tenor saxophonist Paul Gonsalves, who had been with jazz trumpeter and band leader Dizzy Gillespie.

To Ellington, the new members of his orchestra meant a new sound—and that was exciting. Some pieces were written to showcase the new musicians, although without Johnny Hodges the orchestra was missing one of its key players.

The orchestra still found work although most of its performances were for only one night. Ellington's train cars had become too expensive. Instead, his musicians and their equipment now went from city to city in a rented bus. Ellington himself traveled in a car.

Ellington had other difficulties in finding work for his musicians. Not only were there fewer nightclubs than in the past, but most of these were not able to afford the high salaries Ellington required for his large orchestra. This was the early 1950s and small jazz combos were becoming more and more popular. People enjoyed the intimate

In 1955, Ellington was featured on a record called *Rock 'N Roll Revue*, which also spotlighted such stars as Nat King Cole.

sound of a handful of musicians, and the combos were also far less expensive for nightclub managers. Theaters that had once featured live acts on stage—including vaudeville houses— were either shutting down or turning into movie theaters. Times were changing. Duke Ellington remained a celebrated name in the music business, but it was getting very difficult to find places where the orchestra could perform.

Television was becoming increasingly popular with Americans. Ellington tried to make use of the medium, yet jazz and swing music seemed better suited to radio stations than television. Still, television could not be ignored. Whereas nine percent of American homes had televisions in 1950, 87 percent had them in 1960. As TV grew in popularity, movies and radio were on the decline.

Ellington did make several short films for television. About four minutes in length, these short movies included performances of "Mood Indigo," "Sophisticated Ladies" and "Solitude." Ellington also made appearances by himself. Sometimes he would play on the piano and other times he would be a guest on game shows such as "What's My Line?"

The record industry had also changed through the years and now Ellington focused on recording a long-playing record (rather than ones that played for a shorter period of time). "Masterpieces by Ellington" was his first long-playing record and others soon followed, such as "Ellington Uptown in Hi-Fi" and "Ellington '55." Ellington also made a record that highlighted his work on piano. Using only bass and drums on the record with him, Ellington recorded "The Duke Plays Ellington," which was later renamed "Piano Reflections."

Many critics stated that Ellington's best music was behind him with pieces like "Sophisticated Lady." Ellington was aware that the orchestra was not moving forward, yet he was unsure of how to get it back on track. Jobs were sparse in the mid-1950s and Ellington even played background music for a show with ice skaters. This was not the kind of performance he enjoyed, but it was work and it paid. He would not give up.

Chapter 10

Tributes

Just when it was looking bleakest for Ellington's orchestra and career, word came that Johnny Hodges' small band had broken up. Leading a group of musicians had been more work than Hodges had bargained for. In August 1955, the saxophone player returned to Ellington's orchestra.

With the addition of a new drummer, Sam Woodyard, things began to look up. In July 1956, the band was set to perform at the Newport Jazz Festival in Rhode Island. Because of various delays, the musicians had to wait until midnight to go on stage. And when they finally took the stage and performed Ellington's "Diminuendo and Crescendo in Blue," the crowd went wild. Always the showman, Ellington picked up on the audience's excitement and was practically dancing on stage, encouraging his band to give their best as they played more pieces. They did . . . and the performance was recorded by

Columbia Records. The album that resulted from that evening, *Ellington at Newport*, was Ellington's best-selling long-playing record of his career. *Time* magazine ran a cover story on Ellington the following month. Once again, he found himself on top.

Ellington now signed a three-year deal with Columbia Records. The deal was so successful that at the end of the three years, the contract would be extended for three more years.

Ellington had been asked to write a composition for the 1957 Shakespeare Festival in Stratford, Ontario. Ellington wrote "Such Sweet Thunder," which he played for the first time at Town Hall in New York City before performing it in September in Ontario. It was certainly a challenge for Ellington to write music about Shakespeare, but Ellington enjoyed the task. The piece—sometimes called "The Shakespearian Suite,"—met with good reviews. In years to come, Ellington would play selected movements in concert performances.

Ellington and his orchestra returned to Europe in the fall of 1958, visiting England, Scotland, France, Belgium, Holland, Sweden, Norway, Denmark, Germany, Austria, Switzerland, and Italy. While in England, Ellington met Queen Elizabeth. When he returned to the United States, he wrote a composition in the Queen's honor. He would not release the music of "The Queen's Suite" while he was

Ellington was the subject of *Time* magazine's August 20, 1956 cover.

◆◆◆◆◆

alive, but instead gave the one copy he had made to Queen Elizabeth.

The musical *Jump for Joy* had reopened in Florida. Ellington and his musicians traveled there for a twenty-day run. Yet the show lost a large amount of money and had to close.

As Ellington turned sixty, he was asked to write the score to the movie *Anatomy of a Murder* starring Jimmy Stewart and Lee Remick. The album of the soundtrack won three Grammy Awards.

He was asked to write another film score the next year for the movie, *Paris Blues*, starring Paul Newman and Sidney Poitier. Although this score did not win any awards, the background music received a nomination for an Academy Award.

Ellington was honored in September 1959 when he

was awarded the Spingarn Medal by the NAACP. The award is given annually to an African American who has made notable achievements. Ellington took the honor seriously. After performing at Johns Hopkins University, he purposely went to a restaurant in Baltimore, Maryland, that was known for not serving African Americans. As expected, Ellington was not allowed to eat in the restaurant. Since he was a celebrity, this made headlines in the newspapers. Ellington also would not perform at a segregated club in Little Rock, Arkansas, and only played in auditoriums in Dallas and Houston, Texas, after they had agreed to permit blacks and whites to sit together. Never before had these auditoriums allowed their audiences to be integrated.

In 1963, an event was organized in Chicago to celebrate the hundredth anniversary of the Emancipation Proclamation. Abraham Lincoln had issued this document which freed all slaves in the Southern Confederate States during the Civil War. It was considered a major step toward ridding the entire country of slavery.

Ellington was asked to take part in the Century of Negro Progress Exposition. He wrote a composition called "My People," which featured a jazz band, dancers, and a choir. Ellington met civil rights leader Martin Luther King, Jr., while rehearsing this piece.

Ellington spent nearly half of 1963 traveling in Europe. European journalists raved about Ellington's performances.

Not only did his orchestra play at performances across the continent, but he also had recording sessions in France, Sweden, Germany, and Italy, as well as television programs in England and Sweden.

"He nearly always comes out on top," said Toby Hardwick. "You can not [sic] back that guy into a corner. It can't be done. He's got an answer every time . . . The amazing thing about him is that the language, the slant, everything, it's all acquired. It didn't rub off from someone else, and it wasn't a legacy, either. He went inside himself to find it. He's an *only*, that's for sure. They threw away carbons."[1]

In September 1963, Ellington made a tour of India and the Middle East, including Iraq, Iran, and Lebanon. The orchestra created a sensation in Damascus, Syria, where seventeen thousand people flocked to the first jazz concert performed by a big band rather than a small ensemble. Because of this success, a CBS television crew recorded the rest of the tour. The orchestra would return to Europe in 1964 and 1965.

Although in his mid-sixties, Ellington had no intention of slowing down, much less considering retirement.

"What is there to retire to?" he asked. "Stagnation wouldn't look good on me. My band and I travel all over the world, see the sights and see the people. You can't beat that. The road is my home, and I'm only comfortable when I'm on the move."[2]

He was still looking for ways in which to challenge himself musically. In 1965, he was asked to write a piece for the Grace Cathedral in San Francisco, California. "Concert of Sacred Music" used bits and pieces of earlier works, such as "Black, Brown and Beige" and "My People." Although not all critics praised the work, it won a Grammy Award in 1966 as best original jazz composition. In addition, Ellington was given the President's Gold Medal after performing at the Festival of the Arts at the White House in 1966. President Lyndon Johnson went on to appoint Ellington to the National Council on the Arts.

Two television programs were made of Ellington's musical role in the "Concert of Sacred Music," one of them winning an Emmy Award in June 1967. "Concert of Sacred Music" was performed not only in California, but also in New York City at the Fifth Avenue Presbyterian Church. The performance was recorded by RCA Records, and Ellington would go on to perform this composition at least fifty times. On one occasion near the close of 1966, he performed the work in Washington, D.C.'s Constitution Hall. This concert, however, was not very well attended because some ministers in Washington had protested the religious piece as being too worldly.

Still, Ellington did not seem to have lost any of the energy he had as a younger man. "I am the world's greatest listener," he said. "Here I am, fifty years later, still getting cats out of bed to come to work, so that I can listen to them and so that they can make a living for their own families."[3]

As years went on, he lost some people who had been close to him. His wife Edna—they had never divorced—died in 1966. The next year, in May 1967, his writing partner Billy Strayhorn died.

As Ellington approached his seventieth birthday, he remained active, devoting nearly all his attention to his music.

"He has few outlets," said Mercer Ellington. "Some people play golf, swim, or play tennis, but his only interest is music, and he uses his energies to write."[4]

A Tribute to Billy Strayhorn

Billy Strayhorn and Ellington had been working together for more than a quarter of a century at the time of Strayhorn's death. They seemed at times to be able to read each other's minds. Strayhorn had become ill with cancer and soon was no longer able to travel with the band. Before long, he was confined to a hospital bed, where he continued composing music. When Strayhorn died, Ellington was devastated. He said, "Billy Strayhorn was my right arm, my left arm, all the eyes in the back of my head, my brainwaves in his head, and his in mine."[5] He wrote a tribute to his friend and partner and had his orchestra record a piece called " . . . And His Mother Called Him Bill."

Ellington received many honors as he approached his seventieth birthday. He was invited to a celebration at the White House. The guests included Benny Goodman, Count Basie, Richard Rodgers, and many others. At the celebration, President Richard Nixon awarded Ellington the Presidential Medal of Freedom. Ellington told the president, "There is no place I would rather be tonight except in my mother's arms."[6]

Many colleges and universities gave Ellington honorary degrees, including Yale, Brown, and Columbia universities. Outside the United States, Ellington had been honored by the Republic of Togo and Chad. Both African nations issued a stamp in his honor. In Sweden, the two-hundred-year-old Royal Academy of Music asked him to become a member. This was the first time in the academy's history that they had offered membership to a composer whose music was not classical.

In 1971, the orchestra made a huge tour that included Russia, more than a dozen European nations, and then several South American countries. Only months later, Ellington took his musicians to Japan, Taiwan, the Philippines, Australia, and other countries in Southeast Asia.

Approaching his mid-seventies, Ellington chose to write his memoirs as one of his last projects. He was offered $50,000 by Doubleday & Company as an advance. Ellington went to work, and *Music Is My Mistress* was published in 1973.

The following year, he became ill while on tour with his orchestra in the Midwest. He checked into a hospital, where he continued to work, using an electric piano from his bed. Ellington had smoked cigarettes all his life. Now he had lung cancer. The disease spread rapidly and on May 24, 1974, he died. More than ten thousand people attended his funeral in New York City.

From the time he was twenty-four, Duke Ellington had kept an orchestra together—a span of more than fifty years. His music took jazz to a new level.

> Ellington had smoked cigarettes all his life. Now he had lung cancer.

"Music to me is a sound sensation," Ellington once said. "It takes me to new places and experiences."[7]

In 1974, the Duke Ellington School of the Arts was founded in Washington, D.C., to help students who are interested in a career in the arts. The public school has sent graduates to the stage, jazz scene, movies, and dance companies.

On what would have been Ellington's hundredth birthday in 1999, he was awarded the Pulitzer Prize for his musical contributions. Ellington had been recommended for a Pulitzer thirty years earlier, but was rejected because at that time jazz was not considered worthy of the prize.

He had toured with his band from New York to Cairo and had performed with some of the greatest jazz legends, including Louis Armstrong and Dizzy Gillespie. Writing

Two grandchildren of Duke Ellington, Edward (left) and Paul, accept their grandfather's induction into the Ertegen Jazz Hall of Fame at the new Jazz at Lincoln Center in New York on September 30, 2004.

and recording hundreds of compositions, Ellington had played before royalty and presidents.

Ellington himself did not like to label his music. Although considered a jazz composer, he did not approve of labels. He believed "music was good or bad, that was it," said drummer Louis Bellson. "Playing with that band you heard sounds you never heard before. You never knew what to expect, but whatever he did you knew was going to be beautiful. Music poured out of him."[8]

Chronology

1899—Is born on April 29 in Washington, D.C.

1906—First piano lessons.

1913—Begins high school.

1914—Hears pianist Harvey Brooks and becomes interested in music.

1915—Writes his first song, "The Soda Fountain Rag."

1917—Leaves school to become a musician.

1918—Forms his own band and marries Edna Thompson.

1919—His only child, Mercer, is born.

1923—Moves to New York City.

1925—Begins work on show with Jo Trent.

1926—Hires Irving Mills as his agent.

1927—His orchestra begins working at the Cotton Club.

1931—"Mood Indigo" is record of the month for Victor Records.

1933—Takes orchestra on first tour of Europe.

1935—Mother, Daisy Ellington, dies.

1937—Father, James Ellington, dies.

1939—Begins working with Billy Strayhorn. Plays at New York World's Fair.

1941—His musical *Jump for Joy* opens.

1943—Makes debut in Carnegie Hall. He is the first black American to play there.

1956—Plays at Newport Jazz Festival.

1959—Wins three Grammy awards.

1967—Billy Strayhorn dies.

1969—Is awarded the Presidential Medal of Freedom.

1974—Dies on May 24 in New York City.

The Duke Ellington Memorial is at the Duke Ellington Circle in the Harlem section of New York City.

Chapter Notes

Chapter 1. Doing It His Way

1. Stuart Nicholson, *Reminiscing in Tempo: A Portrait of Duke Ellington* (Boston: Northern University Press, 1999), p. 7.

2. Edward Kennedy Ellington, *Music Is My Mistress* (Garden City, New York: Doubleday & Company, Inc., 1973), p. 20.

3. Nicholson, p. 9.7

Chapter 2. Between Music and Art

1. Edward Kennedy Ellington, *Music Is My Mistress* (Garden City, New York: Doubleday & Company, Inc., 1973), p. 10.

2. "Duke Ellington Special: Ellington on Racism," *The Guardian Manchester* (UK), Apr. 16, 1999, p. T004.

3. Ellington, p. 6.

4. Stuart Nicholson, *Reminiscing in Tempo: A Portrait of Duke Ellington* (Boston: Northern University Press, 1999), p. 9.

5. Ellington, p. 33.

6. Ibid., p. 26.

7. Ibid., pp. 27–28.

8. Ibid.

Chapter 3. Putting It Together

1. Stuart Nicholson, *Reminiscing in Tempo: A Portrait of Duke Ellington* (Boston: Northern University Press, 1999), p. 9–10.

2. Ibid., p. 21.

3. Stanley Dance, *The World of Duke Ellington* (New York: Charles Scribner's Sons, 1970), p. 56.

4. John Edward Hasse, *Beyond Category: The Life and Genius of Duke Ellington* (New York: Simon & Schuster, 1993), p. 47.

5. Ibid.

6. Ibid.

7. Dance, p. 62.

8. Ellington, p. 36.

9. Dance, p. 57.

10. Derek Jewell, *Duke: A Portrait of Duke Ellington* (New York: Norton, 1977), p. 31.

11. Ellington, p. 37.

Chapter 4. Back in New York

1. Edward Kennedy Ellington, *Music Is My Mistress* (Garden City, New York: Doubleday & Company, Inc., 1973), p. 69.

2. Nicholson, p. 35.

3. Stanley Dance, *The World of Duke Ellington* (New York: Charles Scribner's Sons, 1970), p. 57.

4. Nicholson, p. 49.

5. Ellington, p. 71.

CHAPTER NOTES

Chapter 5. The Cotton Club

1. Stanley Dance, *The World of Duke Ellington* (New York: Charles Scribner's Sons, 1970), p. 11.

2. "Duke Ellington Special: Ellington on Racism," *The Guardian Manchester* (UK), Apr. 16, 1999, p. T004.

3. John Edward Hasse, *Beyond Category: The Life and Genius of Duke Ellington* (New York: Simon & Schuster, 1993), p. 100.

4. Nat Hentoff, "Happy Birthday, Duke," *The Washington Post*, Oct. 17, 1998, p. A21.

5. Dance, p. 67.

6. Ibid., p. 68-9.

7. Derek Jewell, *Duke: A Portrait of Duke Ellington* (New York: Norton, 1977), p. 45.

8. Jeff Bradley, "Duke Ellington's Life More Fascinating Than Godlike; Sophisticated, Superstitious, Musician Exuded Ambition," *Denver Post*, Feb. 7, 1999, p. K01.

9. Stanley Dance, *The World of Duke Ellington* (New York: Charles Scribner's Sons, 1970), p. 35

Chapter 6. New Horizons

1. Stuart Nicholson, *Reminiscing in Tempo: A Portrait of Duke Ellington* (Boston: Northern University Press, 1999), p. 103.

2. Jesse Hamlin, "Ellington's Genius Is Celebrated on 100th Birthday: He Created a New Kind of American Music," *San Francisco Chronicle*, Feb. 21, 1999, p. 32.

Chapter 7. A Temporary Halt

1. Derek Jewell, *Duke: A Portrait of Duke Ellington* (New York: Norton, 1977), p. 71.

2. Jeff Bradley, "Duke Ellington's Life More Fascinating Than Godlike; Sophisticated, Superstitious, Musician Exuded Ambition," *Denver Post*, Feb. 7, 1999, p. K01.

3. Jesse Hamlin, "Ellington's Genius Is Celebrated on 100th Birthday: He Created a New Kind of American Music," *San Francisco Chronicle*, Feb. 21, 1999, p. 32.

4. Bradley, p. K01

5. Jewell, p. 59.

6. Stuart Nicholson, *Reminiscing in Tempo: A Portrait of Duke Ellington* (Boston: Northern University Press, 1999), p. 164.

7. Nat Hentoff, "Happy Birthday, Duke," *The Washington Post*, Oct. 17, 1998, p. A21.

8. Jewell, p. 64.

9. James Lincoln Collier, *Duke Ellington* (New York: Oxford University Press, 1987), p. 175.

10. Stuart Nicholson, *Reminiscing in Tempo: A Portrait of Duke Ellington* (Boston: Northern University Press, 1999), p. 186.

Chapter 8. Beyond Barriers

1. Derek Jewell, *Duke: A Portrait of Duke Ellington* (New York: Norton, 1977), p. 17.

CHAPTER NOTES

2. Stuart Nicholson, *Reminiscing in Tempo: A Portrait of Duke Ellington* (Boston: Northern University Press, 1999), p. 191.

3. Stanley Dance, *The World of Duke Ellington* (New York: Charles Scribner's Sons, 1970), p. 70.

4. Jeff Bradley, "Duke Ellington's Life More Fascinating Than Godlike; Sophisticated, Superstitious, Musician Exuded Ambition," *Denver Post*, Feb. 7, 1999, p. K01.

5. Edward Kennedy Ellington, *Music Is My Mistress* (Garden City, New York: Doubleday & Company, Inc., 1973), p. 156.

6. Dance, p. 29.

7. Bob Blumenthal, "The Highest Notes: In the Century Since His Birth, Duke Ellington has Been the Most Important Composer of Any Music, Anywhere," *Boston Globe*, Apr. 25, 1999, p. K1.

8. Nicholson, p. 199.

9. John Edward Hasse, *Beyond Category: The Life and Genius of Duke Ellington* (New York: Simon & Schuster, 1993), p. 241.

10. Nicholson, p. 231.

11. Ibid., p. 233–234.

12. Hasse, p. 248.

13. Nicholson, p. 249.

Chapter 9. Changing Times

1. John Edward Hasse, *Beyond Category: The Life and Genius of Duke Ellington* (New York: Simon & Schuster, 1993), p. 284.

2. Ibid., p. 294.

3. Jesse Hamlin, "Ellington's Genius Is Celebrated on 100th Birthday: He Created a New Kind of American Music," *San Francisco Chronicle*, Feb. 21, 1999, p. 32.

Chapter 10. Tributes

1. Stanley Dance, *The World of Duke Ellington* (New York: Charles Scribner's Sons, 1970), p. 61.

2. Derek Jewell, *Duke: A Portrait of Duke Ellington* (New York: Norton, 1977), p. 17.

3. Stuart Nicholson, *Reminiscing in Tempo: A Portrait of Duke Ellington* (Boston: Northern University Press, 1999), p. 446.

4. Dance, p. 42.

5. Edward Kennedy Ellington, *Music Is My Mistress* (Garden City, New York: Doubleday & Company, Inc., 1973), p. 156.

6. Jewell, p. 26.

7. Ellington, p. 299.

8. Jesse Hamlin, "Ellington' Genius Is Celebrated on 100th Birthday: He Created a New Kind of American Music," *San Francisco Chronicle*, Feb. 21, 1999, p. 32.

Discography
A Partial List

Complete Legendary Fargo Concert (Remastered)—2006, Disconforme.

Quadromania—2006, Membran/Quadromania Jazz.

Supreme Jazz—2006, Membran/Quadromania Jazz.

Cotton Club Stomp: 1929–1932—2005, Jazz Legends.

Duke Ellington—2005, Membran/Documents.

Duke Ellington Presents—2005, Shout! Factory.

Ellington '66—2005, Collectables.

Essential—2005, Castle/Pulse.

The Essential Duke Ellington—2005, Legacy Recordings.

The Great Paris Concert (Collectables)—2005, Collectables.

Legendary Big Bands—2005, PULSE.

The Piano Player (Digipak)—2005, Storyville.

Songbook: Mood Indigo—2005, Definitive.

A Sophisticated Genius (Remastered)—2005, American Legends.

The Symphonic Ellington—2005, Collectables.

Will Big Bands Ever Come Back?—2005, Collectables.

Blues in Orbit—2004, Legacy Recordings.

The Centennial Collection—2004, Bluebird RCA.

The Duke Steps Out—2004, Living Era.

Further Reading

BOOKS

Brown, Gene. *Duke Ellington: Jazz Master*. Woodbridge, Conn.: Blackbirch Press, 2001.

Hannah, Jonny. *Hot Jazz Special*. Cambridge, Mass.: Candlewick Press, 2005.

Hill, Laban Carrick. *Harlem Stomp! A Cultural History of the Harlem Renaissance*. New York: Little, Brown, 2003.

Pinkney, Andrea Davis. *Duke Ellington*. New York: Hyperion Books for Children, 2000.

Terrill, Richard. *Duke Ellington*. Chicago: Raintree, 2003.

INTERNET ADDRESSES

Duke Ellington
   <http://www.dukeellington.com>

Edward K. "Duke" Ellington
   <http://www.schirmer.com/composers/ellington_bio.html>

A Passion for Jazz! Music History and Education
   <http://www.apassion4jazz.net/>

Index

Page numbers for photographs are in **boldface** type.